Once they crosse[...] moon and stars li[...] [a] part of Lacy wanted to turn back. But another part of her wanted to go on, to experience anything that might happen, to feel once again the hardness of Sloan's body pressed against hers, to taste the nectar of his kisses. Her wayward side won. Without a word Lacy walked onward, her awareness of Sloan at her side intensifying with each step she took.

That was why, when Sloan stopped and turned to her, Lacy automatically echoed the movement.

As had happened before, primitive necessity asserted itself the instant the two of them touched. And again Lacy was no match for it. Whatever he wanted, she would do. She knew she had only to give the signal and they would stretch out on the coolness of the grass, acting out her fantasy....

R CH...
is also the author
of this title in
Love Affair

GAME OF HEARTS

Passion's Prey

GINGER CHAMBERS

A Love Affair from
HARLEQUIN
London · Toronto · New York · Sydney

First published in Great Britain in 1985 by
Harlequin, 15–16 Brook's Mews, London W1A 1DR

© Ginger Chambers 1984

ISBN 0 373 16071 2

18-0585

Printed and bound in Great Britain by
Richard Clay (The Chaucer Press) Ltd,
Bungay, Suffolk

Chapter One

"It's not like I'm asking you to move to Siberia, for heaven's sake!" The impatient voice vibrated along the long-distance telephone lines. "All I want you to do is come back to Texas for a few weeks."

The dimple in Lacy's right cheek deepened, and her hazel eyes filled with fond amusement at the evidence of her sister's rising exasperation.

"Some people would say that's one and the same thing," she murmured softly, still pretending to resist.

The desired result was not long in coming. Ariel's breath practically hissed from one section of the country to the other. "Well, I knew you had changed, Lacy Stewart, but I never would have believed you could forget so much so fast!" Outrage quivered in every word. "Texas was a good enough place for you to be born and grow up, but now that you've lived in Boston for a few years, you've turned into nothing better than a—"

Lacy decided to intervene. Raising an unseen hand she laughed and called, "Wait! Don't say it! I was only teasing."

Ariel was not easily appeased. "No you weren't. You meant every word. And it isn't as if you couldn't use someplace to go, not after the way that professor you worked with up and died on you."

The sudden silence that followed her outburst made Ariel realize she had gone too far. Richard Evans's death had occurred only six weeks before. It was still too fresh to be spoken of so freely. "I'm sorry," she apologized stiffly. "I didn't mean that the way it sounded. I—"

"It's all right," Lacy returned, her previous humor no longer apparent. "It's the truth."

Another small silence stretched between the sisters. Then Ariel observed, "You've had a pretty rough time of it, haven't you?"

"It hasn't exactly been easy."

"Did you love him that much?"

Unconsciously Lacy lifted one shoulder. Richard Evans had been twenty-seven years her senior, long separated from his wife, the father of two children almost as old as she—and yet he had fascinated her from the first moment he had stridden into the large lecture room where she was a first-year university student, and changed a minor interest in biochemistry into a major one. She had even moved to Boston to be near him when he accepted an invitation to join a prestigious university there. But love him? She thought of the hollowness that was present in her life.

"I must have," she answered huskily at last.

Ariel sighed. Privately she wondered if Lacy knew the meaning of the word *love*. But she had already delivered enough hurt for one day, so she kept the thought to herself. Instead she said, "I really do need you, Lacy."

A sad smile touched Lacy's lips. "Why do I get the feeling that I'm your latest charitable cause?"

"I don't know," Ariel replied tartly. "But I don't appreciate it, not one bit! I've already explained about the chance I have to go with David on this trip. And about Sampson. If you don't come take care of him David will want to put him in a kennel. And the last time we did that he almost died. I'd be worried sick about him every moment I was away. So if you won't come, I'll have to cancel my plans. And a trip to Europe isn't exactly an opportunity that comes along every day of the week."

"Why don't you ask someone closer? There's got to be any number of people in Austin who would jump at the chance."

"Have a stranger stay in my home?" Ariel was shocked. "You've got to be kidding! I'd worry about what I'd come home to, if there would be anything left. I couldn't do that."

"You worry too much."

"And if I didn't, who would?" her sister demanded, sniffing. "You certainly don't seem to care."

Lacy took a deep breath, her inner eye visualizing Ariel as she had last seen her: slender, with flashing brown eyes, a small, slightly turned up nose, a pretty if somewhat wide mouth. She wore her dark brown hair long and straight to her waist, pulled back at the crown with a clasp. It was several shades darker than Lacy's own, which fell only to her shoulders. Two years separated the sisters, two years of rivalry when they were younger. But as soon as each had become adult, the striving for attention lessened and they now could be counted as friends. Yet that fact merely added to the knowledge each had of the other, and Lacy knew that Ariel was trying to maneuver her to her way of thinking. The laying on of guilt had worked before, it would work again. Only this time Lacy was unwilling to put up much of a fight because she had already come to the conclusion that a return to Texas might be a wise move. Boston held nothing for her any longer, not even a job, since the new grant they had received had been cancelled upon Richard's death.

"All right. I'll do it," she agreed, and Ariel's quick intake of breath was followed by an exultant "You will?"

"I will," Lacy confirmed. "When did you say you wanted me there?"

If Ariel had been present, Lacy was sure she would have been almost suffocated with hugs and kisses. "Oh, Lacy, thank you—thank you! Whenever I can do anything for you, just let me know. Oh, I'm so happy! I'll find a present for you in each place we visit." She calmed a degree. "Did you ask when? Well, David's company has already scheduled a meeting for him in London on the twenty-eighth. So, you should be here about the twenty-fifth. Would that be OK with you? You and Sampson can get to know one another again and I can run over the list of things he needs—"

"I'll be there," Lacy interrupted. One of Ariel's worst faults was the six pounds of aristocratic poodle she called Sampson, and if she ever got going on his care and feeding, they would still be talking at midnight.

Ariel gave a blank, "Oh." Then, "All right. I'll make arrangements for your air fare."

"You don't need to do that," Lacy protested. "I have enough money to cover it."

"You're doing this for me, remember? I'll pay. Just don't miss that plane."

"I won't, big sister. And if I have to, I'll get the stewardess to pin a note to my collar so that if I get lost someone will show me the way."

The stiffening of Ariel's jaw was felt, not seen. "There was no need for that, Lacy," she returned haughtily.

"No, I suppose there wasn't," Lacy agreed, smiling gently to herself. "I'll be there on time."

"And be careful."

"I'll be that too."

Two weeks later to the day Lacy was making her way along the aisle of a sleek jet, the ticket folder with her seat assignment stapled to it in one hand, her other hand clutching a carry-on bag and the strap of her purse. She wasn't particularly experienced with air travel, her one trip from Texas having been made with Richard. Then all she had had to do was follow his lead. Now she was on her own and she was beginning to wonder if a note wouldn't have been a good idea, something like a car used for the purpose of teaching a novice to drive being plastered with warnings of its hazardous load. Couldn't airports furnish tags that said "Inexperienced Traveler"?

"Excuse me," she murmured as she came upon a fellow traveler who was completely blocking the passageway as he loaded his possessions into an overhead storage compartment. His broad back moved possibly one inch.

The little slashes of yellow in Lacy's otherwise tan-shaded eyes sparkled into life at the man's indifferent response. She was tired. She had been up for most of last night, her mind active with remembrances of Richard: his patience, his devotion to his work, the pride he had felt on completing his last and most detailed technical paper; of how happy she had been for him then; how she had not minded in the least the hours upon hours of research she had done to help make his publishing a fact, with no credit due herself. Then, like a recurring sickness, she had gone on to relive once again that awful night when the ravaging heart attack had taken them both by surprise as they worked late in the laboratory. His pain, her panic.

Lacy was in no mood to accept any form of insolence, even an insolence that she alone perceived. She cleared her throat and repeated pointedly, "I said, excuse me."

The pale blond head turned until blue eyes that could have rivaled Paul Newman's in clearness and impact were looking down at her. Their irritated expression was a perfect match for her own. The man didn't seem any happier about her intrusion than she was with his. Lacy felt his gaze travel over her before it was transferred back to the compartment above his head. She could have been a pesky fly attempting an attack on the thick skin of an elephant for all the credence he gave her.

She glared at the classically handsome profile that was so obstinately presented to her and felt her irritation increase. "I'd like to get by. Please move!"

At least this time her frigid direction achieved an acknowledgment of her presence. "In a minute," he growled, and the deepness of his voice rumbled through her.

"I don't *want* to wait a minute. If you don't make room immediately, I'm going to call the stewardess." There! Maybe a threat would help.

The next thing that happened was the slamming of the compartment door. The noise sounded like a shot to her strained nerves and Lacy jumped in reaction.

"Far be it from me to stand in your way," the man grumbled nastily as he folded his long body into the aisle seat. Then he bent his blond head to glance at the watch on his wrist, as if timing the seconds until take-off. He was not the least concerned whether she moved on or not.

Lacy drew a deep breath, trying to contain her temper. That was one of the things she had always liked about Richard. He knew how to treat a woman. He was never rude, never demanding. She began to walk further down the aisle. But as she went, the numbers on the seats were all wrong. Instead of getting nearer to her assigned place, she seemed to be getting further away.

She checked the seating slip once again and began to move back up the aisle, against the flow of passengers continuing to come on board. "Excuse me—excuse me," she murmured repeatedly until she began to feel like an inexperienced idiot. She was plunged even further into dismay when a child moving beside her stopped to ask if she needed help.

Lacy looked into the assured green eyes of the rounded face that was loaded with freckles. "Er—" was all she could choke out.

The little girl, who was possibly all of ten years old, took the ticket folder from her unresisting fingers and studied it a moment before pointing. "That's your seat over there. Next to that man with the blond hair.''

Lacy's eyes followed the child's pointing finger and settled with a sense of dread on the occupant of the seat. *Marvelous,* she thought. *Great. We can either growl at each other all the way to Texas or try to pretend that the other doesn't exist.* Either way promised an uncomfortable trip.

She thanked the little girl with a tight smile and moved five rows forward. When she stopped beside the man, she did a quick double check of the numbers herself, but she couldn't force them to change. Maybe she could arrange with a steward or stewardess to find her another seat.

At the same time she was forming that thought, the man looked around to see her standing beside him. His blank expression soon changed to a disdainful sneer, and Lacy's backbone became steel. She had made enough of a spectacle of herself this day; she wasn't about to give him the satisfaction of seeing her do it again. She would sit in that empty seat even if King Kong were her traveling companion. And from the noise the man made deep in his throat as she moved in front of him, she decided the giant ape might be a better option.

Another complication to her already too complicated day occurred when her bag wouldn't fit beneath the seat ahead, and the man, watching her efforts to squeeze it in, complained, ''That's definitely not going to work. You'll need to stow it away.'' With an irritable motion of his head he directed her attention to the compartment above them.

Lacy wanted to make a horrible face at him. He was

acting so superior. Did he practice making himself objectionable, or was it just a natural talent? She returned shortly, "I was just waiting for the rest of the people to come on board—so I wouldn't be in the way." It wouldn't hurt to let him think about that not so subtle little dig.

"Wait too long, and there might not be room close by. This flight looks as if it's booked solid."

Lacy rested the bag on her knees. "That's my concern, not yours." She dismissed him coolly.

From the corner of her eye she saw him give a light shrug making the material of his dark jacket move with the solid-looking muscles that lay beneath. "Don't say I didn't warn you," he admonished hatefully.

A scowl settled on Lacy's normally pretty face and her soft lips tightened, yet she said nothing. She didn't want to be responsible for a continuation of the conversation between them. There are some people you meet that you like immediately. Then there are those you instantly form an aversion to; and you don't know why, you just do. Well, he was one of the latter. And she had no intention of furthering their acquaintance, if it could be termed that. As soon as she secured her bag, she would bury her nose in the news magazine she had purchased in the airport gift shop and not come out of its pages until the jet landed.

As the stream of boarding passengers lessened and the muted sounds of conversations blended with the warming hum of jet engines, Lacy turned away from her prolonged study of airport activities and decided to brave the aisle to find a spot for her carryon bag.

"Good luck," the man murmured sarcastically as she once again passed before him, straining to avoid even the slightest measure of physical contact between them.

Just on the off-chance that there would be room in the area designed for use by their seats, Lacy reached up to release the overhead compartment door. She found that he had filled the entire space with his possessions: a leather luggage case took up the bottom shelf and a matching attaché case, along with a tennis racket and sports bag, took up the other. Lacy let the door swing shut with a decided snap. Didn't he have any other luggage? Or had he carried it all on board with him in total disregard for other passengers' needs? She sent the carved lines of his arrogant face a killing look and privately decided that his nose was too straight, too perfect, that it needed a hump or something to give it character.

For the next five minutes Lacy searched for somewhere to put her bag. Finally it took the stewardess's assistance to locate an empty area, and that had to be above the child who had helped her earlier. Lacy suffered the little girl's pitying look with a forced, confident smile, while all the time her insides were fluttering with shame. She was a university graduate, a top honor student. She had completed her bachelor's degree in three years and gone on to attain her master's in biochemistry by the time she was twenty-two. Then she had been an assistant to Richard for the following four years, delving into various fascinating aspects of genetic research. And she was totally at a loss in this atmosphere. A child of ten was more seasoned!

With her cheeks a little pinker than usual, Lacy made her way back to her seat. The man gave a muffled groan as this time she managed to step on his toe. Lacy was too mortified to acknowledge his pain. Maybe if she pretended that she hadn't noticed—

But he didn't let the moment pass. "God, I'm glad you don't weigh a lot!" he declared caustically.

"Did you say something?" Lacy inquired innocently, hating him for being there.

Eyes the color of a clear summer sky looked across at her, silently waiting for an expression of regret. But at her continued blank look he retreated back into the newspaper he had been reading, straightening it with a pointed rustle.

Lacy fastened her seat belt and took a deep, silent breath. She rescued her magazine from the safekeeping of her shoulder bag, which she had secured beside her on the seat, and tried to become involved in the problems of an article on nuclear proliferation as explained by a brilliant mind. But the whine of jet engines and the beginning movement of the plane as it taxied to takeoff position broke her concentration, and her quickened heartbeats began to reflect the approach of anxiety.

When Richard had been sitting beside her, he had quieted the fears that she patently knew to be groundless. More people were killed in automobile accidents every year than in air crashes; she knew the words. But somehow, sitting in a tiny tube that was about to catapult itself into space, statistics took a back seat to primeval emotion. Her fingers tightened on the edges of the magazine that lay in her lap.

All through the moments leading to takeoff and the actual event itself, Lacy kept her eyes closed. If they were going to crash, she didn't want to see it. She didn't open her eyes until they were safely in the air, and then when she did, she happened to glance out the

window and saw that the earth was tilting crazily as the
pilot made a tight banking turn. She couldn't help her
instinctive frantic lean the other way, as if by her tiny
effort she could counterbalance the weight of the air-
craft and keep it from flipping over.

Of course the man by her side was amused by her action. And since she had unconsciously pressed against
his shoulder in her alarm, she could feel the silent
laughter he was doing little to hide.

"Is this your first time to fly?" he asked tauntingly,
maddeningly.

Lacy immediately straightened, although it was like
pushing against a terrible force. The plane still seemed
to be resting on its side as it cut through the sky. Her
eyes remained glued to the horizon and only when it
finally began to straighten was she able to pull them
away and answer, "No, usually I get on my broom
every full moon!"

If Ariel were here she would undoubtedly tell her
that that had been another uncalled-for remark. But
Lacy didn't care how unfriendly she sounded. She just
wanted to be left alone, particularly by the person at her
side.

Laughter exposed the man's very white, very even
teeth. Really, if he wasn't so obnoxious, he just might
be the most breathtakingly attractive man she had ever
seen. The thought ran through her mind to wonder if
he were some kind of model. He certainly had the
looks to be one: manly and virile, yet with that spark of
mocking humor that might be considered irresistible by
some women. But not by her, of course.

"Is that spelled with a 'w' or a 'b'?" he asked at
last.

"What?" Uncomfortably Lacy realized she was staring at him and dragged her eyes away.

"As in 'witch' or—"

"I was thinking more along the lines of 'Why don't you mind your own business?'" she interrupted frostily, her lips tightening in disapproval.

"You really want me to?"

"I'd like nothing better."

He raised an estimating eyebrow that was several shades darker than his hair, as if gauging the seriousness of her statement. It seemed that whatever had been causing him to act so grouchy had been left on the ground in Boston. And now that he was ready to greet the world, she was elected to be the one he reached out to.

Well, he could just think again, Lacy fumed to herself. Her mood wasn't any better; her problems weren't so easily wished away. Richard had been the hub of her life for so many years she couldn't begin to stop missing him so quickly, even if she wanted to—which she didn't.

The strength of her conviction must have been more than apparent because his smile instantly faded and a short "OK, if that's the way you want it" followed. He turned his attention back into the columns of his newspaper, while Lacy adjusted her reading material into a more comfortable position.

Minutes later she was still having a hard time losing herself in the complexities of the article. She was much too aware of the man sitting next to her—of his long frame that was lounging so easily on the cushion beside hers, of the way his clothing fitted his slim, taut body, of his long, finely-shaped muscular legs.

When the time came for the stewardess to run through the emergency procedures, Lacy listened intently to every word. But she noticed that the man did not. Either he didn't care about what to do if the jet suddenly developed trouble, or he had flown so frequently that he could have given the memorized spiel himself.

When the small lecture was over, Lacy went back to her article. She was just beginning to make progress, learning the ratio of missiles and warheads positioned in various parts of the world when it was time for service of their meal. With some relief she put the disturbing material away and concentrated instead on getting the food tray into position before her. Soon the stewardess assigned to their section approached.

"Oh! Hello again, Dr. Adams," the attractive redhead exclaimed as she paused from taking the warming cover off a tray of steaming food. "It's so nice to see you again. Did you have a nice visit in Boston?"

Doctor? Lacy's head came up a degree as she heard the title, but she kept her eyes studiously averted. He was a doctor?

"Pretty good," the deep baritone answered.

"And how was the convention?"

"Like conventions usually are, I suppose—exhausting."

"Now, you can't tell me you didn't have a little fun, too," the stewardess teased with easy familiarity. "I won't believe you if you do."

Lacy let her glance move casually sideward as the stewardess slid the tray into position before him. For all anyone could tell, she was just checking the makeup of the meal being served. In actuality, she was examining the man once again. Was he a PhD or an MD? No, definitely not a PhD. But then he certainly wasn't her idea of a medical doctor either. They were supposed to be old, or at least older, with lines marking their faces from all their interrupted sleep at night. And, most of all, they had to have kind, understanding eyes—not sky-blue chips of ice one minute and devilishly mocking ones the next.

The aroma of food tickled her nose as a tray was placed before her. Then when they had settled on their drinks, they were left alone to dine.

The breast of chicken resting on a bed of wild rice was tempting to Lacy. She had been too keyed up about the coming flight to eat breakfast this morning, but she couldn't force herself to swallow one bite until she made a small observation.

"So you're a doctor. Funny, I wouldn't have believed it. Have you injured anyone with your bedside manner lately?"

After a so sweetly phrased question that seemed to come from nowhere, the man put down the fork he had just freed from its plastic prison and turned to face her. Lacy felt the burning touch of his eyes, although she wouldn't meet them. She pretended to be involved in cutting her piece of chicken.

"I haven't had any complaints," he murmured at last.

"Isn't there an old saying about a lost patient being a silent patient?" The need to irritate him further drove her on. She still was experiencing some resentment against anyone in the medical profession for not having saved Richard's life.

After a small silence the man commented smoothly,

"You really do have a grudge against the world, don't you?"

Lacy's color heightened, but she refused to answer. She was being a bitch, just as he had earlier tried to say, but she couldn't seem to stop herself. She gave an uncaring shrug.

"In answer to your question," he went on stiffly. "I do lose a patient occasionally. All doctors do. But my patients couldn't complain even if they wanted to. I'm not a medical doctor, I'm a veterinarian. I treat animals."

If it were possible to discover a convenient hole to fall through in an airplane, Lacy wanted to find one. And if she didn't fit completely, she would gladly sacrifice her mouth since it seemed to be the most troublesome part of her anatomy.

The man watched her for a moment, then turned back to his meal. Lacy remained mute, suddenly having lost all desire to eat.

The strained silence that radiated between them for the hour and a half remaining until the scheduled stop in Houston was one of the most uncomfortable periods Lacy had spent in some time. She knew she should apologize. Knew he would probably accept it, if only to antagonize her. But she couldn't make the words pass her lips. And her magazine didn't help at all. The rest of the articles were just as depressing and intense as the first.

The landing in Houston was uneventful, the pilot barely letting the plane bobble on touchdown. As soon as they taxied to a stop, the man next to her unclipped his seat belt and walked away without a backward word or glance, leaving Lacy to wonder if he would request a change of seat for the last leg of the flight. He had left his possessions, so that meant he was not going to depart here.

Much to her surprise he came back a short time later, dropping with casual unconcern into the seat beside her, a men's magazine, *Playboy*, in his hand.

He saw her quick glance at what he was holding and confided dryly, "Don't worry. I only look at the pictures."

At that outrageous claim—the exact opposite of what most men say when confronted with the fact of their reading preference—Lacy was amazed at his audacious action. He had probably chosen that magazine just to see how she would react.

Well, she wasn't about to let him think he had disconcerted her. Gathering a measure of surface sophistication she returned in a bored manner, "Oh, me too. Only I much prefer *Playgirl*."

Blue eyes twinkled from beneath golden brown lashes as a fine spray of wrinkles touched their corners.

"Each to his own, I suppose."

Lacy pretended to become lost in another article. She wished she had had the sense to disembark and buy something else to read herself, but if she tried to do it now—with her luck—the plane would probably take off without her. She tried not to notice that he both looked at the pictures *and* read the articles.

The forty-five minute flight to Austin was over before she fully realized that it had begun. This time either the pilot didn't bank the plane so sharply or she was too caught up in other thoughts to notice. At any rate they were soon taxiing to the gate.

Without waiting for the airplane to come to a full

stop, some of the people began to gather their possessions from the overhead storage areas. Dr. Adams was one of them. He swung his bag onto his empty cushion, fished out his attaché case, put his tennis racket under his arm, and hooked his sports bag over one shoulder.

As he was accomplishing this, Lacy was again made unwillingly aware of him—of the long lean body his opened jacket revealed, of the finely tuned yet not overly obvious muscularity. She quickly turned to look out the window when he was finished; she didn't want him to catch her staring.

She felt his eyes dwell on her for a moment before he drawled, "I suppose I should say that it's been nice meeting you."

Lacy turned slowly to confront him. "Only if you mean it," she returned coolly. Why was she feeling so darned uncomfortable, as if she alone had been the cause of their breach of decorum.

"Then I won't," he decided, making her blink.

Lacy's chin went up. "Neither will I."

His response was a short laugh and a flash of even white teeth. Then, as their forward motion halted, he hoisted his case from the seat and turned to walk up the aisle.

Lacy's eyes followed his wide shoulders and blond head until she couldn't see him any longer. Only then did she think about getting her own bag.

Her late start resulted in her being one of the last passengers off the plane. And when she entered the luggage claim area, her temporary companion on the flight from Boston was nowhere to be seen. If he had any additional luggage he had already collected it.

Lacy gave a tired sigh and wondered at the cause of her malaise. The only reason she could fathom was that it was a loneliness of spirit because Richard was no longer with her.

Chapter Two

The building that housed the main offices of Dr. Sloan Adams and his partners was located in an affluent area some distance away from the heart of Austin itself. It had been constructed only five years before and contained every state-of-the-art device that any doctor who dealt in the treatment of animals could possibly want. Rarely did any person or animal cross its threshold who did not have a high degree of perceived blue blood running through his veins.

But that office was not the only veterinary practice the partners operated. The other was the exact opposite, at least in outward position and appearance. It was located in a run-down section of the city, and seldom did any of the beings who used the clinic have any pretension to regal ambitions.

Of the two Sloan Adams much preferred the honesty of the second. The area had been his home as well for the first seventeen years of his life, and he was well acquainted with it. It was to this office that he went before making his way to his apartment.

Jenny, the office assistant, looked up with a start

when he came into the reception area. "Dr. Adams!"
she cried with both surprise and delight.

Sloan gave a crooked smile. "You were expecting
Dracula, maybe?" he teased, giving a credible imita-
tion of Bela Lugosi's foreign accent.

A heated blush rose to flood the young woman's
cheeks. She was in her late teens and Sloan had known
for some time that she had a bit of a crush on him, so
he treated her as an affectionate older brother might
and waited for the case of puppy love to fade.

Jenny's eyes were a much darker shade than her
brown hair, and the slight accent to her speech was a
heritage of her Mexican birth. "Oh—no. I—I just
thought..."

Sloan came further into the room, his smile gentle.
"It's OK, Jenny. I'm back a day early. Is Jim around?"
This reference was to his oldest partner, the man who
had inspired him to follow him in his work.

"Yes, he's with a patient now, but it shouldn't take
long. It's just a parvo booster."

As the last word left Jenny's mouth a door a short
distance down the narrow corridor opened, and a little
boy came out carrying a rag of a dog in his arms. He
was followed by an aging man wearing a pale blue lab
coat and sporting dark-rimmed glasses on a face that
spoke of years of loving concern. The man was deep in
conversation with the boy. He didn't look up until they
were in the small lobby, then his blue eyes widened
behind the magnified lenses of his glasses.

"Sloan—? What are you doing here?" He stopped
walking, causing the youngster to stop with him. Then
he frowned. "Wait a minute. What day is today? I

haven't lost another one, have I?'' Absently he patted
the child on his back signaling that he could leave. The
boy flashed a grin and ran out the door. "I'm getting so
damned forgetful lately," Jim Stanton complained, his
forehead creasing even more. "No. I'm right. It's Tuesday. And you're still supposed to be in Boston, at the
convention."

Sloan smiled fondly as he watched his old friend
come to his accurate conclusion. "I couldn't stick it
another day, Jim. I warned you that either you or Max
should go. You'd probably have enjoyed it more."

"And you didn't?"

Sloan gave a short laugh. "I'm here, aren't I?"

Jim began to shake his head. "I don't know what I'm
going to do with you, son."

Sloan's smile increased. "You've said that before."

"But this time I mean it. Although"—he took the
glasses from his nose and put the end of one wing into
his mouth to nibble on before taking it out to motion
with when he was again ready to talk—"I could never
really stand those things myself. And Max told me
years ago that if I ever tried to make him go again he'd
quit. I guess that means we're all just a bunch of stick-
in-the-muds."

"So, I'm not going to be fired?"

"Did you think you would be?"

"Hell, no."

The older man came slowly across the room and
placed an arm about the younger man's shoulder, his
face warm with affection. "Come on. I want to show
you something. It's that little white pup."

Sloan followed in his friend's footsteps and listened
as he rambled on about the little dog that had been

found near starvation a few days before his departure for Massachusetts.

"He doesn't look like the same animal!" Sloan approved when they arrived in the small hospital area and Jim stopped in front of a cage containing a snowy white dog.

"Nope, he doesn't. Eats like a pig."

Sloan hunched down on one leg and put his fingers through the wires. Immediately the bright-eyed little puppy of mixed breeding began to lick them with his soft pink tongue, his tail swishing happily in greeting.

Sloan was tired and vaguely out of sorts from the unsatisfying days he had spent in the crush of people at the convention. But upon being so forcibly reminded of the worth of his chosen profession, some of the dissatisfaction with the political infighting he had witnessed over the past few days began to disappear, and a small glow of happiness returned to his heart.

Jim Stanton began to chuckle. "I think we can thank Jenny more for his recovery than anything I did. She's back here with him every chance she gets. I wouldn't doubt that she's going to adopt him permanently as soon as we say he can go."

Sloan smiled and tickled the underside of the dog's chin before straightening. Then, for some reason, the face of the woman who had shared the journey home with him came into his mind. Her hair was almost the same shade as Jenny's, only a little longer, and her skin was a creamy shade of ivory, which made her big hazel eyes, busy flashing resentment, show up even more. He hadn't understood why she had showed him such hostility, but he had sensed the hurt behind her action. That was one of his talents as a vet. As he had told her,

animals couldn't speak to tell their doctor where their
pain was located, so he, along with most other practi-
tioners in the field, had developed the deep ability to
empathize, to feel. It was like a sixth sense. And with
her he could sense both confusion and pain. Like a hurt
animal, she had struck out.

Not that he had exactly been a sweetheart himself,
he remembered wryly. He had been so busy nursing
his own anger over the waste of three days' work that
he had acted like a grizzly bear disturbed in hiberna-
tion.

Also in his memory was the slimness of her body
and the way her soft blouse had clung to the twin
rounded thrusts of her breasts. He could still smell the
delicacy of her perfume.

"Sloan?" The older man's voice broke into his
thoughts and gave Sloan a mental jerk. Why had he
remembered her just then? He didn't even know her
name. Talk about an exercise in futility! He had already
settled on the woman he was going to marry; he had
known her a long time. It was her father who was
calling him. "Sloan, did you hear me?"

"Oh, yes. Yes, I hear you. I was just—thinking of
something else."

Jim took the message wrongly. "Don't let it bother
you, son. Neither the time nor the money was wasted.
You learned something from the experience."

Sloan let the idea stand. He shrugged. "I guess that's
all any of us can do."

"Correct. Now"—Jim broke into a wide smile—
"does Caroline know you're back?"

A flower-like essence wafted to his senses. He forced
it away. "No."

"Then why don't you come home with me and give her a surprise?"

Sloan bent down to give the puppy's head a final rub. "Sure. Why not?"

"Good. Good. I'll tell Jenny she can leave early."

All during the drive to Ariel's home, Lacy's past was constantly being refreshed in her consciousness. She hadn't thought she had missed Austin, but now that she was seeing it once again, she found that she had. In four years little had changed. The state capitol was still the same, it's rounded dome reaching into the sky. The University of Texas could be seen spreading over blocks of land. Town Lake was as beautiful as ever, the houses on a short cliff beside it adding to its allure. Familiar sights flashed by one after the other: the various state offices of a multitude of Texas organizations, the Holiday Inn, the Denny's Restaurant—and soon the dry rocky hills that gave grudging life to mesquite and stunted oaks came into sight as the sisters left the city proper behind.

Ariel spent the time talking constantly, but Lacy listened with only part realization of what was being said. And when they pulled into the driveway of her sister's home, she could not have repeated even a portion of it. She thought most of it concerned Ariel's excitement about the coming trip, but she couldn't be sure. Memories, like shadows, had clouded her perception.

"Now tell me," Ariel demanded after she came around the back of her parked car and stood before Lacy's open door—her pride plain to see as she surveyed the modern architecture of her home—"how do you like what we've done since you were here last?"

Lacy stepped out of the car and narrowed her eyes

against the bright July sun. The house still looked the same. It was a contemporary dream of rough cedar boards, brick, and glass. But where, before, the front yard had been a replica of all the others nearby—barren because of newly finished construction—it now was a veritable garden. Trees had been carefully placed and highly mulched beds rose from timbered outlines, where shrubbery vied for position with summer blooms. In the spaces where beds had not been placed, a thick lush carpet of grass could be seen. No expense could have been spared to create the effect.

"It's—breathtaking" was all Lacy could manage. In truth she wasn't sure how she felt. She had always loved the wildness of the outskirts of Austin; she had never been sure that she agreed with the taking of sections of what had once been rugged rangeland and turning them into tame subdivisions.

"David and I love it!" Ariel exclaimed. "All we really have to do now is see that it's kept watered."

"I can imagine," Lacy murmured in return. Now *that* was an understatement if she ever heard one. With the heat of a Texas summer upon them, she didn't want to think how much water would be required to keep everything alive. But she was afraid that she was probably going to find out.

As if reading her younger sister's mind, Ariel said, "Of course you'll have to water every morning while we're away, but you won't mind doing that—will you? David is going to have an underground sprinkler system installed as soon as he can. We should have had that done first, but"—she laughed self-mockingly— "you know us. We didn't think about needing one until we already had everything else in place."

Lacy gave a wry grin. "It seems to run in our family to do things the hard way."

Ariel took the step that separated them and coupled her arm with Lacy's. "Mom always said that it did. I guess she was right." She began to move forward down a cobbled pathway, Lacy in tow. "It's good to have you back home, Lacy. I've missed you."

"Like missing a case of the measles?"

Ariel's brown eyes sparkled with mischief. "Or the mumps." Then she hugged her sister's arm. "No, really. I've worried about you way up there in Massachusetts." She hesitated. "Do you think you might move back down here, now that..."

Lacy had prepared herself for that question, knew it would eventually come. Yet she had not found a satisfactory conclusion. She hedged on giving a committing answer. "I don't know, Ariel. I'll have to think about it. And, right now, I don't want to think very much."

Ariel nodded her understanding. "I can see that," she said softly. Then she brightened again. "Sampson's going to be so happy to see you. He's missed you too."

Lacy gave a soft groan to herself. What her sister needed was something else to lavish her attention on. She was positively batty over that dog! "He probably won't even know who I am," she disagreed.

Ariel laughed. "He's been sleeping with your picture for the last two weeks. I thought that might help."

Lacy could scarcely believe her ears. Her sister *definitely* needed to go on this vacation. But she said nothing, and when they entered the house, she was surprised that the little silver-gray poodle did seem to remember her. Either that, or he acted as if he loved everyone he met, which she suspected was more the truth than was the length of his tiny memory.

"See, what did I tell you?" Ariel proclaimed.

Lacy made sure that her answer was garbled as she fended off a flurry of licking dog kisses to her face.

The hours before her sister's departure were spent receiving repeated instructions. And by the time she saw Ariel and David off to the airport in a taxi—they had insisted on her not driving them—Lacy felt as if she had been put through some kind of an emotional wringer. She had enough names, numbers, and directives to fill a small book, all listed in just-in-case order starting with the telephone number of Sampson's vet.

That last information had given Lacy a small jolt. She didn't know much about the man who had journeyed with her from Boston other than the facts that he was a veterinarian and that he had left the plane in Austin, which was enough, considering the number of times a vision of him had unwillingly projected itself into her mind. But she didn't want to know more. So she had experienced a vast amount of relief when she saw that the poodle's doctor's last name was Dalton.

His had been Adams. She wondered what went with it. Stuart? Lance?

Lacy promptly gave herself a good, firm talking to. She had to stop thinking this way! He was nothing to her, just an unpleasant encounter that one has occasionally. She would probably never see him again.

For the next couple of days everything went beautifully for Lacy and Sampson. Away from her sister's smothering presence, Sampson was discovered to have quite a

fearless personality. In fact, it was his newfound belief
that he was a greyhound instead of a gray poodle that
caused him to come to grief.

Lacy had started out that Sunday morning, just as
she had all the previous days, by watering the massive
lawns. Sampson had watched her progress from behind
the living room windows as she worked in the front
yard, running from one window to the next in order to
get a better view. Then, when she moved to the rear of
the house, she had let him come outside to frolic about
the fenced-in yard. He seemed to be enjoying his vacation as well as his owner was probably enjoying hers.

The accident happened as they were coming back inside the house. His little paws must have been damp,
because when he scooted past the rear patio door, intent on racing Lacy in, his feet skidded on the polished
kitchen flooring and he went sliding across the room
until he was stopped by a hard smack against a heavy
wooden table leg. After giving a terrified, "Yipe!" he
tried to stand. But even as he did, his hind leg crumpled
beneath him and he fell back to the floor with a pained
cry.

For a moment all Lacy could do was stare at him,
stunned by what had happened so quickly. But she
soon shook off the feeling of incredulity and hurried
across to the little dog's side, a rush of fear for his wel-
fare supplanting any thoughts of what Ariel might do to
her for allowing the unthinkable to happen.

Liquid black eyes looked up at her from the small,
gray-plumed face. "Oh, baby!" Lacy cried, wanting to
touch him but afraid to. "What have you done to yourself?"

She didn't care that she probably sounded a great

deal like her sister right then. Almost from the first day of their reacquaintance the little dog had wormed his way into her heart, and she couldn't stand to see him suffering.

Her hands were trembling as she finally reached out to examine his injured leg. She could tell nothing, all of his bones felt terribly fragile. He was so very small. A whimper met her efforts, and Lacy stopped. She didn't want to do anything to hurt him more.

On legs that felt suddenly like well-cooked spaghetti, Lacy located the book of instructions she had received from Ariel and dialed the number given for the vet. While impatiently waiting for the ringing telephone to be answered she stretched the coiled cord as far as it could go and dropped down onto the floor beside the stricken poodle, smoothing the curly hair at his throat. He seemed to appreciate that she was trying to comfort him.

Finally the connection was made, and Lacy's heart gave a gratified leap, only to plunge into instant dismay when she discovered that the voice on the other end of the line was nothing more than a recording. Lacy's grip on the receiver tightened and she felt like crying. Then, as she remembered what day of the week this was, her impotence increased. This was Sunday! Would any veterinarian's office be open? Through the haze of her uncertainty she heard the voice drone on to state that if there was an emergency she should call another number. The number was imprinted on Lacy's brain.

Quickly she stumbled back to her feet and redialed. Again it took several rings before the telephone was answered.

"Vet Emergency Clinic," a voice said.

A rush of relief flooded Lacy's body. As long as she

had gotten through to a live person, a good deal of her problem was over.

"My sister's dog has been hurt!" she blurted out, her voice high and strained.

"OK. Tell me what happened."

Lacy took a deep breath, the masculine voice on the other end of the line lending her assurance.

"He slid into a table leg and now he can't get up. I think he may have broken his leg."

"Do you have a way to get him to the clinic?"

Lacy thought of the car left in the garage for her use. "Yes."

"Do you know where we're located?"

"No."

"Are you by yourself?"

Lacy seemed to be specializing in short abrupt sentences. "Yes."

"Then listen closely, and calm down. Your dog will be all right."

He was talking to her as if he thought her much younger than her actual years, but Lacy didn't correct him in his assumption. At the moment she felt younger. Give her an organism, any organism, and she could tell you its makeup and purpose of life on the planet. But with a living, breathing fellow being in a state of agony...

She memorized the instructions as he gave them. The clinic was located in the city itself.

"I'll be there just as soon as I can. Er—" She looked down at Sampson's fuzzy face. "Is there some special way I should pick him up? I mean—"

"How big a dog is he?"

"A toy poodle."

The doctor gave a short chuckle that somehow sounded familiar, but Lacy was in no state to wonder.

"I think you should be able to handle him. If you can find a board, put him on that. If not, just pick him up carefully and try to keep him still. I'll be waiting for you."

The drive into the city was grueling. Lacy found a board and had placed Sampson on it, but she worried about each bump in the road and kept one eye on the highway ahead and one on the suffering dog.

The directions took her into a poorer area of the city. Lacy's mind's eye absorbed this, but since she was certain she had followed the instructions correctly, she didn't hesitate or waver in her resolve. She was intent on only one thing: getting Sampson's pain relieved.

The building that housed the emergency clinic was neat if not exactly new, and it was sporting a recent coat of fresh white paint. Lacy stopped the car in a graveled parking lot and hurried around to the other side to slip Sampson and his board from the seat. She then carefully made her way across the loose surface, all the while making soothing noises to the now silent dog.

When she came to the door, she paused, uncertain how to open it. She didn't want to jostle Sampson any more than she already had, and she wasn't about to put him down, so there seemed only one way to solve the problem. She raised one still-damp tennis shoe and thumped the thick wood as hard as she could. Her action brought immediate response. The door was opened by a tall blond man who, in Lacy's eyes, seemed to fill the entire entryway.

Sloan Adams stood rigid at the door, his right hand

forgotten on the knob as he suffered the shock of having the woman who had persisted in invading his thoughts over the past days standing before him. In that moment a rush of thoughts shot through his brain. On the plane he had termed her pretty, but on closer inspection, in the natural light of day, she was more than that. She was beautiful. Not even the washed-out jeans and old plaid shirt she now was wearing could detract from the classical lines of her features. Her gleaming chestnut hair was mussed, as if the wind had been playing games with it, and her stunned hazel eyes were hard to look away from. He felt an immediate sensual drawing toward her. He wanted to reach out and touch the soft skin of her cheek, smooth her lips with his thumb and follow that with his mouth. But a tiny whimper from the dog she was holding forced his attention away from physical urges, and with relief he slid back into his role of healer.

"Here, let me take him," he stated gruffly, turning his words into fact.

Lacy's fingers were lifeless appendages when Sampson was taken away from her. Now she knew why that laugh had sounded familiar. It was he! A mass of confused emotions rumbled through her body. One part of her wanted to jerk the dog away and find another clinic. Surely there were other vets in town. But another part, the saner part, knew that her wish was purely selfish. She couldn't put Sampson through more agony while she searched.

"Are you coming in or staying out there?" the hateful voice she remembered thundered in her ears. Why was he yelling at her? Lacy shook herself to complete awareness, only to realize that he wasn't yelling—it had just sounded that way as his words echoed through the jumbled recesses of her mind.

"I'm coming in, of course," she responded crisply. Didn't he remember her? There had been no form of recognition in his expression.

"Then do it, and close the door behind you."

Lacy did as she was directed and followed his wide-shouldered back as he moved down a short hall into a treatment room. Maybe he didn't remember her, but she certainly remembered him. It would be almost impossible to forget the disagreeableness of his character. Was he only willing to be friendly at 30,000 feet?

By the time Lacy rounded the doorway, the man had Sampson placed on an examination table and was gently, expertly, running his fingers along the dog's hurt leg and hip.

"He slid into a table leg?" he asked, his striking blue eyes rising to jab into her.

"Yes. We had just come in from watering—" For some stupid reason she wanted him to know that she didn't usually dress in this type of clothing, that she had just donned it to care for the yard.

"I don't believe anything's fractured," he cut in. "I think he's just dislocated his hip, but we'd better take a couple of X rays just to be sure." His interest in her explanation as to where they had been and what they had been doing was absolutely nil.

Lacy stifled the words that begged to be given life. She watched as again Sampson was lifted and transported into the hall. The little dog whined in pain, making Lacy's conscience twist because for a moment her pride had taken precedence over his need.

"Don't stay in there," the doctor's voice called as he

walked away. "I'm all by myself, so you're going to have to help."

Lacy again had to fight to keep silent. He had to be the rudest man alive! Couldn't he just ask? Surely he knew she would do anything she could to help. Why did he have to go out of his way to be offensive?

"What do you want me to do?" she asked as she found the room he had moved into. Outside was a radiation warning sign and inside was a conglomeration of equipment; she had no idea what purpose each served.

"Stay over there for a minute, then you can come put one of these on." He motioned to a pair of heavy lead aprons that were hanging on a hook attached to the wall.

When Lacy's eyes swung back to him, she found that his gaze was fastened upon her. But as soon as she met his look, he turned to the table, his back concealing what he was doing as he crooned softly to the frightened animal.

As Lacy waited, she found that even in these circumstances she couldn't avoid her awareness of him as a man. He had the kind of long, lean body that spoke of fitness and basic masculine appeal. His legs were long and supple, his hips and waist trim, his back and shoulders possessing a smooth muscularity. He was dressed in dark slacks and a cotton pullover shirt, and as she had thought once before, he could have been a representative of a modeling agency. But there was something more about him than just the way his body was put together. It was an indefinable something, a sexual fascination that seemed to speak louder than his antagonizing attitude. Lacy was not immune.

"Okay," he spoke over his shoulder. "Come do as I said." He must have been privy to her every move because when she hesitated at the strangeness of the weight of the apron, he said, "It slips over your head. Go on, it won't bite."

Lacy couldn't prevent a muttered defensive, "No, but you may!" that she hadn't meant for him to hear. Yet he did. She looked up into a pair of amused blue eyes.

"I've had my shots," he assured her, then laughed when a disgusting pinkness brightened her cheeks.

She sent him a killing glance and tied the apron strings at the back of her waist. As far as being a ravishing garment went, the apron left a lot to be desired. But since she wasn't here to seduce anyone, she was happy for her dual protection.

"I've inserted a tube down his throat for anesthesia," he warned, suddenly becoming businesslike again. "So don't be upset when you see it. He was in a lot of pain and this will make taking the X rays easier. Then if his trouble is just a dislocated hip, I can pop it back into place while he's still asleep."

Lacy clearly heard what he was saying as she approached the table, but she still was not prepared for the sight of Sampson's small body lying immobile on the large flat surface, a plastic tube, which was connected to a nearby machine, coming out of his mouth.

"Are you all right?" the doctor asked as she wavered slightly.

"Yes—I'm fine." She had to swallow twice in quick succession. That must have been what he was doing when his back was to her.

A dark gold eyebrow quirked estimatingly; then as

she became steadier, he directed, "You'll have to wear lead gloves, too, because we have to hold him steady."

Lacy nodded, her eyes glued to the quiet gray body that only moments before had been aware.

The man moved away, and a few seconds later he came back wearing his own lead apron. He handed her a pair of heavy gloves, then pulled his on at the same time as she did.

"OK. Now, we're going to take two pictures, one on his side and one on his back. You hold his front feet; I'll position his rear."

Feeling more and more as if this were some sort of dream, Lacy complied. She had never expected to be here, with this man, doing this kind of work, when she awakened this morning. How was she ever going to explain the situation to Ariel? Without conscious thought, her fingers curled.

"Not too tight," she was advised. "Just keep him steady."

Chastised, Lacy relaxed her grip. She held her breath when a small button on the floor was depressed and the X ray machine came to life.

"OK, good. Now, on his back."

It was fortunate that Sampson was able to sleep through the ordeal of stretching him out tummy-side-up. If he hadn't been, he would have thought they were torturing him.

Within seconds the last picture was taken and the vet was arranging the lax gray body into a more comfortable position, still keeping the anesthesia hose connected.

"What happens now?" Lacy questioned.

Electric blue eyes met her wide hazel ones. "I develop the film."

"Will that take long?"

"About ten minutes."

Lacy glanced at Sampson. "Do you want me to stay here—with him?"

"Since there's only room for one person in the dark room—"

"I'll stay here."

For some reason Lacy was almost sure he would have offered to let her come along if it hadn't been for the unconscious dog.

"I'll just get things started," he said easily.

"All right."

She felt his eyes run over her, making a lightning-quick assessment of her features. Then he moved in the direction of a side door, and after discarding the apron and gloves, disappeared within the concealed room.

Lacy gave a trembling sigh of relief when she was at last alone. He seemed able to turn the aspects of his personality off and on like tap water. One minute he was a grouch, sarcastic to a rather cutting edge, and the next he was exhibiting a mocking humor that made her very much aware of the sensual side of each of them. Lacy didn't know how to sort him out. Or if she wanted to sort him out. What she really wanted to do was get out of there, go back to Ariel's home, retreat behind the jade-green living room curtains. But with Sampson in the state he was, there was no doing that.

"Are you still wearing that thing?" The deep voice created a small earthquake along her nerves as it came unexpectedly from close behind. Her blood leaped when fingers came out to tug at the back of her waist. Then the heavy material was lifted away from her slender frame. Next came the removal of the gloves. "We're done taking pictures. You can relax."

Relax? Hah! She wasn't going to relax until she was far away from him. That thought made her feel even more uneasy. Richard had been the beacon of her life. He had been all that she lived for. The time she spent working on projects for him and with him, listening to his dreams, had not been for nothing. She had loved him, wanted only the best for him, had ached for him all the times when he was disappointed or disturbed. Wasn't that love? But she had never been aware of him in exactly the same way as she was aware of the man. And she felt disloyal.

Her eyes flickered up to examine the vet as he checked Sampson's well-being. He was so gentle with the dog. Did he reserve his softer side for the animals in his care? Her gaze wandered over the golden strands of hair that were styled in a perfect razor cut and grew to medium length against his neck. His hair was thick and soft-looking and had just enough of the darker gold beneath to be authentic. But somehow, the thought never occurred to her that he might bleach it as some men did, and she knew that the gentle curl that swirled each end was real as well. Not for Dr. Adams was the fashionable men's permanent.

A bell sounded nearby and prompted him to return to the dark room. Within a few seconds he was out again.

"The films are in the fixer. It'll be about five more minutes till they're ready." He came to stand by the counter and leaned back against it, his arms folding in a relaxed manner over his hard, flat stomach. As his gaze narrowed on her speculatively, he observed, "Don't you think it's time you told me your name? All I've gathered about you so far is that you don't like to wait, you appreciate the artistic merits of *Playgirl*, and you have a sister who owns a poodle with a problem. Now, I admit that's quite a bit, but I'd like to know a little more.''

Chapter Three

So he did remember! He had known all along and kept the knowledge to himself.

"I don't see that my name is all that necessary," Lacy returned stiffly, unwilling to admit her surprise at just how much he did recall.

"It would be nice to know who to bill."

"I'll pay cash."

"I have to have it for my records."

Lacy glared at him.

"Do you have an answer for everything?" she challenged.

"Not everything."

"But you do for this."

He shrugged. "I have to comply with the rules."

"Which means I have to as well."

"Do you have some reason for not wanting to tell me?" Sloan watched her steadily, wondering at her hesitation. He had sensed her confusion and pain before. Now he felt it again.

Her chin went up. "No."

"Then?"

"It's Lacy—Lacy Stewart."

A slow smile creased his cheeks, and the nerve endings throughout Lacy's body vibrated to attention.

"Now that wasn't so hard, was it?" he murmured.

Lacy pulled her gaze back to Sampson. She was all messed up inside. She didn't know what was hard and what wasn't. She just wished the X rays would get finished, so they could find out the extent of the little dog's injury and then she could get away. She would transfer his care to his own vet tomorrow.

"Where do you live?"

The question insisted on following her thoughts.

"I'm visiting."

"Your sister," he deduced. "Do you live in Boston?"

Lacy had taken about all she was going to take. Her hazel eyes flashed upward to meet his amused gaze. "I don't see that I need to answer that at all. It can't possibly have anything to do with your records."

He uncrossed his arms and pushed away from the counter to begin a slow advance across the room. "No, but like I said, I'm curious about you."

Lacy's heart rate doubled as he drew near. But when he stopped at the table, the dog being his target, not her, she felt a mixture of foolishness, relief, and nervous disappointment. The last emotion increased her anger and she took it out on him.

"Aren't those X rays ready yet? Are they going to take all day?"

"Are you in a particular hurry?" He cocked his blond head to one side.

Lacy looked away. Everything she did seemed to make matters worse.

"You know, you should slow down more," he went on to say. "For your own good, you should learn to relax."

"Are you prescribing for me, too?" she asked sweetly, her smile fixed.

"I'd have my license taken away if I did. No, what I'm talking is good common sense. You always seem to be in a such a rush, and with the size of that chip on your shoulder..."

Lacy drew a quick breath to counter that assertion, but before she could begin her defense, the crackling air between them was shattered once again by the sound of the bell.

"Hold onto that thought," she was advised.

While Lacy was alone her mind seethed with a variety of thoughts, none of which would have been printable in a scientific journal, or in any kind of journal for that matter.

The temperature of the room could have dropped to below freezing by the time Sloan returned to the table. He even felt an imaginary chill run along his spine. Maybe he shouldn't have said that about the chip, but it was true. And he wondered at its cause.

"It's not broken." He spoke into the weighted silence while running his fingers along the sleeping dog's coat. "He just popped it out of joint, so all we have to do is pop it back in. If you want, you can wait outside."

Lacy would not have budged for the world. She watched as the doctor's deft fingers made exactly the right moves, and soon he was disengaging the tube from Sampson's throat.

"He'll be awake shortly."

"And then we can leave?" she asked tightly.

"You're in a hurry again," he reminded.

Sparks struck in Lacy's yellow-brown eyes. "Yes," she replied through gritted teeth.

"You have an appointment?"

"Yes." She didn't exactly lie. She had planned on making a small meat loaf for lunch, and it was woefully past her time to eat, especially when she had skipped breakfast.

"Then you'll be a little late."

"What do you mean?"

Sloan looked into her resentful eyes and smiled. He really was acting the devil, but he didn't care. Something about this woman intrigued him, made him want to make her take notice of him no matter how angry he had to make her to achieve his goal.

"You can't take the dog for another hour."

"What?"

"I thought I spoke clearly. You can't take—what is his name anyway?"

"Sampson," Lacy answered automatically.

Sloan's smile deepened. The names people gave their pets! "Sampson can't be released until I'm sure that he's taken the anesthetic well."

For a moment Lacy was speechless. Then she burst out, "You're not serious!"

"I'm afraid I am."

"But—"

"Would you like to make a call? There's a telephone in the front office."

She blinked. Who was she supposed to call? She wasn't nearly ready to speak to Ariel yet. Oh, he meant her fictitious appointment! Lacy shifted uncomfortably from one foot to the other. Damn, he would have to catch her out!

"No. No, I don't—"

"Won't your sister be worried?"

"She doesn't know yet." The words escaped before Lacy could censor them. She had been so glad not to have to admit her misrepresentation that she had admitted something worse.

"Doesn't know?"

Lacy grimaced. "She's in London, on her way to Paris. I'm dog-and-house sitting."

"Oh."

"Yes, oh." Lacy echoed in a higher octave.

"And your appointment?"

She paused then said, "Was with a meat loaf!" There. If he had to know, he might as well know it all.

For a moment the doctor seemed disconcerted. Then an amused chuckle started deep in his throat and fought its way to freedom and to the maturity of a full-blown laugh. Lacy looked daggers at him as he thoroughly enjoyed her admission.

"A meat loaf!" he repeated, and Lacy wanted to strangle him. He chuckled some more; then, pulling himself together a degree, he said, "I can't leave the clinic, or I'd offer to take you to lunch, but I do have a ham sandwich I brought from home. I'll be glad to share."

"No, thank you," Lacy responded frigidly.

"I'll throw in some chocolate chip cookies."

Somehow Lacy refrained from telling him what he could do with his cookies and declared instead, "I'm not going to wait here another hour." She checked her wrist watch. "I'll be back at one thirty. That should give Sampson enough time."

"I think it would be a good idea if you'd wait a few minutes until he regains consciousness."

At his sudden seriousness Lacy hesitated. "A few minutes?"

"From the look of him I wouldn't say more than that. He's already starting to come out of it."

As Lacy's gaze traveled to the table she saw that what the vet said was true. Sampson's nose was indeed starting to twitch and his feet to wiggle as if he were experiencing a dream. Then slowly his eyes tried to open, only to close again almost immediately.

The doctor went over to examine him. "Yes, he's coming around."

"But you still want to keep him."

"I think it would be advisable."

"All right." Lacy moved closer to the table, careful to avoid any contact with Dr. Adams as she slipped into position on the other side. "Sampson?" she called softly. "I'm here, baby. How are you doing, sweetheart?" She felt the vet's eyes upon her bent head, but she didn't raise her own to meet them.

The little dog's tail thumped weakly once or twice, and he turned his head, trying to focus on her face. "I'm here, honey." She petted the silky hair at his cheek. "I'm here, and you're going to be just fine."

His soft pink tongue touched her wrist before his muzzle dropped back to the table. He seemed to drift into sleep again.

Lacy looked up questioningly. "He is going to be fine, isn't he?"

A muscle pulled in the doctor's cheek. "Yes." This was said softly, almost huskily.

Lacy allowed a small, relieved smile, willing for the moment to make a short peace, since he had helped the dog. "Thank you," she murmured equally as softly.

The doctor's shoulder lifted wordlessly, his gaze intent. A strange tenseness seemed to radiate in the space between them, and Lacy was unable to look away from his eyes. They seemed to hypnotize her. There was a growing, smoldering heat in them that captivated her senses, that made her want to forget there was a table between them, made her want to be gathered in his arms and pulled against his hard chest, made her want to feel his lips against her own.

A quickly indrawn breath alerted Lacy to just how far her unconscious thoughts had taken her. She pulled back both mentally and physically, although she was still shaken by how strongly her emotions had run.

"I—I have to go."

The vet said nothing.

"I—" Without giving another backward glance Lacy hurried from the room, her cheeks afire because she was afraid that he might be able to tell what she was thinking.

Once Sloan was alone he inhaled deeply and then let the breath go in a long, slow release of dammed-up tension. He had never been so close before to throwing reason to the wind, to taking what by all rights was not his to take. He had wanted her then with all the intensity of his being, had listened not to his mind but his body as it cried out for sensual satisfaction. He looked down at his hands and saw that they were trembling. He felt as if his entire body was trembling.

As a result of her unsettled nerves, Lacy shied away from any further thought of food. If she had once entertained the idea of stopping at a fast food restaurant for a quick hamburger-to-go that she would bring to a quiet area to eat to help pass the time, she now drove straight to the nearest park she remembered. It was located directly in the center of downtown Austin across from the Governor's Mansion, a small, pocket-sized area that gave a respite from city streets and traffic. The land was partially sunken, with huge oak trees providing shade, and lush grass covering the hard ground like a carpet. A large gazebo was placed to one side of a path and it was to this that Lacy fled to regain her normal composure.

What exactly was happening to her? she wondered as she took a seat on the low bench outlining the structure's raised flooring. She couldn't be attracted to the man, could she? No! It was impossible. She didn't even like him. A person had to like before she could feel any deeper emotion—didn't she? Like and admire? She had felt both for Richard almost immediately upon meeting him, and their relationship had developed into a warm kind of understanding. But with the man! Lord, she didn't even know his first name or if he was married. She didn't know anything about him.

Lacy was twenty-six, yet there were times when she didn't feel it. Almost since she could remember she had channeled her ambitions into education. She was one of those people who had made straight A's all through grade school, intermediate school, and then high school. In college she had done no less. Learning had always come easily to her. But had it come at a price? In the past she hadn't thought so. She had been content to go out on occasional dates. But if there had been a choice between doing a science project and going to a football game, the science project always won. Then she had met Richard and even though some things had changed—he took precedence over everything else—her life was still involved with academics because his was, and she could have her love of learning blend with her love of him.

It was only since his death that she had begun to question the wisdom of living such a narrow life. Things happened that she had no idea how to handle. At the funeral, when Richard's children had accused her of monopolizing their father's time, of keeping him away from them because of her fear that she might lose some of her control over him, and finally—the most hideous injustice—of keeping their parents from reuniting, she had been devastated. It hadn't been like that at all! But she was at a loss as to how best defend herself. She had been living in Richard's shadow too long, letting him have too much control over her.

At first that idea had been hard to accept, but as the days turned into weeks and she was forced to function without him, she began to wonder.

And now this problem. How did she go about solving it? The man seemed to fascinate her, or at least he fascinated her unconsciously. A tremor passed over Lacy's body as the projected memory of his face and form took shape in her mind. Tall, blond, assured. He was the exact opposite of the man she had given her life to for so long. And he was young. Somewhere around thirty, she would guess. Much younger than Richard's fifty-three.

Lacy leaned her head against a wooden support and tried to steady her distressful breathing. Logically the way to go about this would be never to see him again. But she had to in order to regain possession of Sampson. Lacy gave a small moan that caused a woman strolling nearby to give her a strange look.

What was she going to do? Could she go back to face him again and pretend that nothing had happened? That seemed the only way. Yet was she strong enough to do it? Yes, she decided, she was. She was discovering new reserves of strength and character in herself every day. She would just need a plan.

In the past, every time he had spoken she had reacted to his personality with a surprising loss of inhibition. He seemed to know just how to arouse her least endearing side. Even when he was silent he bedeviled her. So, possibly, if she whipped up a proper amount of simmering animosity she could keep her real confusion of spirit a private awareness known only to herself.

With that resolve Lacy raised her head and forced herself to begin to absorb the beauty of the park. And this time when her stomach protested that nourishment had been too long denied, she stood resolutely to her feet and marched back to her car. She would eat a hamburger, darn it. And she would even enjoy it. She would look upon it as being a kind of fuel that would help her get through the approaching ordeal at the clinic. Lord knew she was shaky enough inside at the prospect of again being in the doctor's company, she wasn't about to show further signs of weakness because of a simple metabolic low.

One half hour later Lacy turned into the clinic's parking area. Before getting out of her car, though, she had to quell a momentary sense of panic and reinstill her hard won veneer of confident disdain. Unconsciously her back straightened and her chin lifted, the classical lines of her face becoming cool. Then she took a deep breath and released the door handle. Her facade lasted only the distance of the pathway, because as she let herself into the office, she walked into what could only be described as pandemonium.

An elderly woman was propped in a waiting room chair, her head lolling unconsciously to one side, a small terrier yapping excitedly on a taut leash she held in one unknowing hand; a cat was hissing in a chair just beyond the dog's lead; and as Lacy stood in the doorway with her mouth falling slightly open in surprise, a harried masculine voice called to her shortly to either have the decency to shut the door or get out. Even while she stood there, a small blue bird swooped low over her head as if intent on a bombing mission, and almost escaped outside. Two small children came rushing up in pursuit just as Lacy quickly closed the door, keeping the bird trapped within. Both of the little girls were screeching and giggling as they tried in vain to catch the elusive budgerigar. When the small blue flash zoomed away down the hall and into the first examination room, the children followed, delighting in what to them was a game.

To the doctor in whose clinic the entire episode was unfolding this seemed to be no laughing matter. There was not even a hint of a smile on his chiseled face as he hurried across to the unconscious woman and knelt down on one knee to take her pulse.

"Well, at least she's still with us," he muttered almost as if to himself.

"What happened?" Lacy asked, still feeling some shock.

The yapping dog made another lunge at the cat, which only arched its back and hissed all the louder.

"God only knows. Here, can you come sit with Mrs. Thompson?" The sky-blue eyes turned on her, and Lacy couldn't find it in herself to refuse.

"Of course. What do I do?"

"Just keep her from falling out of the chair. She's probably going to sue us for everything we've got already, but if I can prevent further injury, we just might stand a chance."

Lacy came to take his place beside the woman. He handed her the limp wrist, then took two long steps and whisked the outraged feline from the chair. The cat rewarded his efforts by immediately wrapping around his arm and digging its claws into the vet's exposed flesh. Lacy thought she heard a strong expletive, but she wasn't sure, since the dog was even more excited at the prospect of losing his quarry.

Just as soon as the doctor moved out of the reception area to put the cat in a cage, the bird flashed by and tried to fly through the paneled wall opposite Lacy's head. After suffering a resounding thump, it flapped its wings a few times as it spiraled to the floor where it stood, weaving drunkenly, blinking its eyes. The children immediately pounced on it, and Lacy feared even more for the bird's life as they began an argument over who was to hold it.

The return of the vet coincided with a low groan from the woman at Lacy's side.

"Oh...Oh...Where is it?" a gravelly voice filled with dread asked. "And where is TuTu? Has that horrible snake eaten him?"

"Snake?" Lacy repeated, her wide gaze going to the doctor.

He gave a pained smile. "It's been put away, Mrs. Thompson, and TuTu is right beside you."

Almost as if on cue the dog issued another series of sharp barks, and the woman struggled to sit upright.

"Oh, TuTu, TuTu," she twittered, gathering the terrier into her arms and hugging him like an infant. "My baby!"

The two little girls finally decided who was going to hold the bird, purely on strength alone. Lacy dreaded for the winner to open her hands, but when she did the bird didn't look much worse for the wear, except that it was panting, its little wings pulsing in and out as it tried to get air.

"Doctor Adams, look!" the winner pleaded as she kept a firm grip on the bird's feet. "Look at Bird! He flew into the wall! Is he okay?"

The vet examined the proffered bird. "I think so. He's probably just a little stunned."

"But is he all right?" the other girl insisted.

"Now he'll never lay an egg!" the apparent owner wailed.

"No, I don't think he will," the vet laughed after a short pause. "But then he never would. Only females lay eggs."

"I knew that!" the first little girl insisted.

"So did I!" the second concurred.

"Doctor Adams!" the senatorian voice of the older woman interrupted.

"Yes, Mrs. Thompson?"

"I must insist that you examine TuTu. I wouldn't have come all this way to have you check him if I didn't feel there was something wrong with him. He's been acting strangely all day and he's barely eaten more than a bite of food."

"All right, Mrs. Thompson, bring him in to the second examination room."

"Is that where the snake is?" she demanded.

Lacy saw the devilish grin the vet tried to hide. Why did she have the suspicion that if he had dared, he would have sent her in with the snake on purpose?

Instead he answered patiently, "No, Mrs. Thompson. The snake is back in the box where he belongs."

"It's a good thing," the woman replied superiorly. "A snake of all things—here!"

The thought ran through Lacy's mind to wonder where else a snake would belong if it was sick, but she kept her lips firmly shut. She wasn't about to dip her oar into this particular tempest.

"I'll be with you in just a moment," the vet insisted. The woman took the hint with an aggrieved sniff and rose majestically from her chair, her bright-eyed dog seeming to be laughing on her arm.

"Now for you," the doctor turned back to the two six-year-olds.

"We're sorry, Dr. Adams," one apologized quickly. "We just wanted to find out whether Oscar was a girl or boy. We couldn't tell."

"Just like we weren't sure about Bird," the second chimed in, only to be elbowed soundly by the first.

Lacy watched the man's face as a smile flickered about his mouth at the admission.

"Why don't you two come back later and I'll help you, OK? Take Oscar and Bird, and I'll let you have your cat later when you come again."

"Oh, he's not our cat, Dr. Adams," the first contradicted. "He just followed us here."

The doctor gave a quiet moan and looked at Lacy, a

mixture of expressions mirrored on his face. Prevalent was the question: do you see what my life is like?

The waiting room was quiet after the little girls left. And while the doctor was examining the terrier, Lacy sank into a chair.

Her wait didn't last long. Soon she heard the familiar masculine voice assuring the gray-haired woman, "I'm sure he'll be fine, Mrs. Thompson. In all likelihood he probably ate something that didn't agree with him. It might have been the quiche."

Lacy blinked. Quiche?

The solid form of the woman emerged, the dog tightly in her possession. "If you say so, Doctor. And thank you. I'll try not to bother you again while you're—here. I'll wait until—"

The rest of her sentence was cut off by the vet. "It was no bother, Mrs. Thompson. Any time."

Mrs. Thompson gave Lacy a snooty glance and then marched through the doorway. Sloan watched her leave, her back stiff with displeasure. She probably would never enter these doors again, he thought, but then maybe he wouldn't want her to. The office in the suburbs was more her style, along with all the other pampered animals and their owners. It would be a rare thing for two little ragamuffins from the street to drop by unexpectedly in that office and want to know whether their pet snake and bird were girls or boys. That was something else he liked about working out of this office—its unpredictability.

He slowly let his gaze turn to the woman who remained. She was still as beautiful as he remembered, and a jolt something like an electrical spark shot through him.

"Your arm is bleeding," she said softly, reminding him.

Sloan looked deeply into her eyes, not feeling the scratches, not even aware of where they were. He shrugged, and from somewhere spoke the words, "It's not very bad."

"It doesn't look very good."

Sloan pulled his eyes away from hers to examine the scratches. They were deeper than he had thought and more extensive. It was a miracle that Mrs. Thompson hadn't fainted from the sight of his blood, but then Mrs. Thompson was more concerned for her dog than for people. His mind skipped on. He would have to confine the cat, keep it for the required ten days.

"I don't mind waiting while you put something on it," Lacy offered, breaking into his thoughts.

Lacy—he liked that name. It had been on the tip of his tongue ever since he had learned it.

Lacy didn't understand why she was so concerned, unless it was because, with everything that had happened since coming back into the office, she could see that he had been through enough. She didn't need to play her hand; she could afford to be magnanimous.

The doctor took her up on her offer. He gave a slow smile and told her he would be right back. When he returned it was with a freshly antiseptic-sprayed arm.

"Sorry for letting you walk in on something like that. It doesn't happen every day, thank God. But I was glad you were here. For a minute there I thought I was losing control."

Lacy couldn't prevent the smile that came to her lips. It caused her dimple to deepen. Another understatement. "It's OK, I didn't mind."

She felt his eyes move over her. "I suppose you're ready for Sampson now."

Her heart was beginning to pound in quicker time, his nearness having its usual effect.

"Yes."

She tried to control it, tried to control the speed of blood flowing through her veins.

"I need to ask a few more questions for my records." It was as if he was warning her, not wanting her to think he was just being nosy or curious.

"All right," she agreed.

He moved over to the reception desk and withdrew a clipboard from its middle drawer. "OK, now your name is Lacy Stewart, correct?"

"Correct."

"And you live at—or your sister's address is?"

When she told him the street name and number, she noticed his fingers pause for a second and wondered at the cause, but the hesitation was only slight before he wrote down what she said.

"Do you know Sampson's veterinarian's name?"

"Dr. Max Dalton."

He wrote that down.

"Do you know him?" she asked curiously.

The vet nodded, keeping his eyes on the paper. "And you're going to pay cash?"

"Yes."

He named his fee for the emergency care, and Lacy opened her purse to pay.

"You're not married?" he asked suddenly.

Lacy glanced up, surprised. "No. Are you?" She could have ripped out her tongue for that one, but since it was already said, she braved it out.

"No," he answered slowly.

If she was to be in for a penny she might as well be in for a pound. "What's your name? Just so I can tell Ariel."

"Sloan Adams."

Lacy nodded. His name was unusual, but she liked it. Somehow it fitted him.

"You should take Sampson in for Dr. Dalton to check tomorrow," he advised. "Just for good measure."

Again Lacy nodded.

"And telling your sister isn't something you should put off. Would you like for me to talk with her, reassure her?"

The offer startled Lacy. "Oh, no! I—I can do it myself."

"You didn't seem very anxious to earlier."

"That was because I wasn't sure how he was going to be earlier. He is all right?"

Sloan Adams's blue eyes smiled. "Of course. I'll go get him."

When Sampson was carried back into the room, he looked as if nothing untoward had happened to him, but the vet warned, "He'll need to be kept fairly quiet for the next week or so. And if his hip becomes extremely painful, it might mean that his leg has popped out of joint again. So keep an eye on him—not that I need to tell you that."

Lacy reached out for a dog who was very grateful to see her. She fended off a bevy of loving kisses.

"No, I'll watch him."

"He'll probably be sore for a time, too. You can give

him some of this." He wrote out a prescription. "Or an occasional half-aspirin."

"All right."

Lacy didn't know what to say next, so she started to turn toward the door.

"Don't forget to visit Dr. Dalton tomorrow," he reminded her.

"I won't," she agreed, "and thanks."

She gave him a shy smile before hurrying out of the building and down the path to her car, her earlier unease increasing because he had been revealed as being so human and almost nice. Somehow it was easier to deal with him when he was a boor.

Sloan watched her departure from the doorway, watched the gentle sway of her hips as she walked down the sidewalk and into the parking lot. And he knew that tomorrow, when she brought the dog in for Max to see, he would be there. He wouldn't be able to stay away.

Chapter Four

Caring for Sampson was easier than Lacy had thought it was going to be at first. When he was awake, he seemed to enjoy the role of invalid, demanding a great deal of lap sitting, petting, and a tremendous amount of sympathetic loving. But most of the time he was asleep, which, Lacy decided, was probably the easier way for each of them to get through this experience.

On Monday he was still sore and limping badly, and Lacy placed the call to Dr. Dalton's office. She had decided to put off calling Ariel until after the dog had been seen by his own vet. She was working on the premise that her sister would be less upset if she had more than the sole opinion of Sloan Adams.

On thinking the man's name Lacy gave her head an impatient shake. Why was it the more she tried to put his image from her mind, the more she seemed to dwell on him? He had been in her thoughts before falling asleep last night and she had awakened to a vision of him this morning as well.

Lacy collected her shoulder bag from the hall table where she had left it the evening before and went to scoop Sampson carefully from his curled position on the velvet sofa.

"Come on, boy," she murmured softly. "Let's get this over with as quickly as we can. And maybe then we'll be able to put our lives back to normal."

As soon as she said those words, Lacy realized that she had no idea what normal was. In academia normal was long hours of pouring over books, pressure about maintaining grades, gaining the desired grants, months of patient, painstaking research, while all the time interacting with other people who lived the same kind of insulated lives, intent on educational and professional perfection. But here, here was freedom. And Lacy didn't quite know what to do with it. In fact Sampson's accident had given her purpose. Caring for the dog this morning had provided something more that she could do after watering the garden, other than wandering about the large house like some sort of long-lost survivor who was unsure of what she should be doing now that she was rescued.

The veterinarian office Lacy drew the Buick to a stop in front of was the exact opposite of the one yesterday. A great deal of tinted glass, strategically placed exterior wall rock, and conscientiously cared for landscaping made it aesthetically pleasing to the eye. Inside there was also a great contrast. There was no chance of chaos here. The colorful plush seats that lined the waiting-room walls below pictures of prize-winning dogs and cats were guarded by the cool, watchful eye of a receptionist, who looked as if she might be able to smile if a precise joke were told at just the right moment—*and* if she thought it was funny, which was doubtful.

When Lacy gave her name and the purpose of her visit, there was a flicker of interest, but not enough to maintain a conversation. Lacy moved to take a seat, keeping Sampson on her lap in as comfortable a position as she was able to make for him. A lick on her fingers was his expression of grateful appreciation.

There was not a long wait before a large man of about forty stepped into the room. He was wearing a blue lab coat and sported a tremendous bushy black beard that blended in with his equally woolly head. His small dark eyes surveyed her first and then centered on Sampson.

"All right, mister," his deep voice boomed. "Just what have you been doing to yourself?"

If the directness of the doctor's question was supposed to make Sampson cringe, it had the opposite effect. The little dog knew the loud voice and responded to it by giving a sore greeting. It must have hurt to wag his tail, because he gave only a couple of short, quick swishing movements, where before he had always tried to wind the fluffy extension off.

The doctor rubbed the wiggling head and long, silky ears, and then spoke to Lacy. "I'm Max Dalton and you're—?"

"Lacy Stewart, Ariel Armstrong's sister."

"Nice to know you, Miss Stewart." He thrust out one large hand for Lacy to place one of hers within. When he let her have it back, her hand definitely knew it had been shaken.

"Would you like to tell me what happened? I've had a report but…"

Lacy gave a small frown. Did veterinarians communicate so quickly? If they did, they probably could teach human doctors a thing or two.

"Yesterday morning Sampson slid into a chair," Lacy began, then went over the entire episode, leaving nothing out. Well, almost nothing. She wasn't about to tell him her reaction to Sloan Adams. Nothing would ever drag that out of her.

"Come into treatment room B. I'd like to take a quick look-see," she was told when she finished.

Lacy followed the large doctor across the pristine linoleum flooring. She placed Sampson on a narrow table that was attached to one side of the wall.

Again competent fingers ran over the injury, feeling for any signs of trouble. When he was seemingly satisfied, Dr. Dalton switched his rubbing motion to the poodle's neck, at the same time fastening his dark eyes on her. Then he asked a question about the injury that Lacy didn't understand.

"I'm sorry," she apologized. "I—"

Somewhere beneath the bristly beard the man's lips must have quirked into a smile. She knew this from the slight movement of the concealing hairs and the twinkle that suddenly appeared in his eyes.

"That's all right. Wait just a minute and I'll have an answer." He turned his head toward the door that led into a rear hallway, and yelled in a somewhat subdued roar, "Hey, Sloan. Come in here a minute."

Lacy started when that name passed his lips. Sloan? Here? But how?

The tall, broad-shouldered form of the familiar vet slipped into the room from the connecting hall. His eyes held Lacy's and he smiled slightly, almost mockingly. Lacy didn't know whether he was directing that derisive acknowledgement at her or at himself.

"Did you need something, Max?" he questioned softly, all the while his gaze maintained possession of hers.

"Yes, the X rays."

"They're in the folder."

"They are?"

"Sure—" His attention was pulled away, and Lacy almost felt like slumping in relief. "Right here. I put them in myself."

Max had the grace to laugh. "And I call myself efficient. If it had been a snake it would have bitten me."

Lacy felt Sloan's amusement. Was he remembering the snake of yesterday too?

"Just be glad it wasn't poisonous," he suggested wryly. "I don't think we have an antidote." His gaze shifted back to her.

"Hello, Lacy."

Lacy swallowed a tight lump in her throat. She didn't dare try to speak. Instead she gave a quick nod.

Sloan let his eyes wander over her. Today she was dressed much more as he remembered her from the flight, in a soft aqua-colored dress that clung in exactly all the right places. He felt a surge of awareness and knew that it had been a mistake to come. He had known it as soon as he walked through the office door this morning. Today was supposed to be his day off, after Sunday duty at the clinic, but he couldn't just turn around and leave. And then he had heard Lacy's call and been trapped, not so much by his colleague's curiosity as by his need to see her again.

"You did a good job on Sampson's leg, Sloan." Max's voice pulled him away from his thoughts. "It could have been tricky."

"Thanks," he murmured almost absently.

Max looked from one to the other, his eyes narrowing before dropping back to the dog. "Well, I think that's about all, Miss Stewart. I'm sure Sloan, here, told you what to watch out for and how his treatment should run so I won't bother to repeat it." He paused. "How did Mrs. Armstrong take the news?"

Lacy's cheeks had brightened because of the way Sloan was looking at her, but at Dr. Dalton's question the rosy hue increased.

"I was waiting to tell her until after I talked with you."

She felt Sloan's gaze narrow. "Didn't you trust me?" he asked softly.

Lacy lifted her chin. "Yes."

"Then?"

Max interceded. "She probably just wanted to be able to tell Mrs. Armstrong I had seen him, Sloan. Was that what it was, Miss Stewart?"

"Exactly." Lacy took refuge in the defensive mechanism of resentment, but she had a harder time stirring up the emotion than she did yesterday. Still, she was able to achieve a commendable glare.

When her eyes flashed with dislike, Sloan's interest grew even higher. There was a fire in her that was a challenge to him. With some calculation he shrugged as if her opinion didn't really matter, and he was satisfied to see that the action only served to irritate her more.

"Is that all, Dr. Dalton?" Lacy asked tightly, afraid that if she stayed any longer she was either going to hit Sloan or reach out to touch the golden smoothness of his hair. And she was appalled at the thought of doing either.

"Yes, I think so," Max Dalton decided, "unless you want to add something, Sloan?"

The corners of Sloan's lips drew upward. If only his good friend knew! "No, not now."

"Then I guess that's all, Miss Stewart," the heavier man concluded bracingly. "Don't hesitate to call us if you need us."

'Lacy nodded shortly and reached for Sampson, only to be stayed in her effort by Sloan's arm. The wrist he held was motionless, but that was no indication of the clamor of senses taking place within her. Her outward body was the only thing not speeded up and heightened by his touch.

"I'll carry him for you," Sloan offered.

She was incapable of making any kind of response, much less of denying his offer. She felt as if she had been struck by a raw, elemental force of nature that left her mute, but oh, so very much alive! What would it be like if he did more?

The trip through the waiting room was a blur for Lacy. She was aware of her feet moving and of the receptionist's interested glance, but she could have been a ghost wafting in a surrealistic mist for all the reality those few seconds held.

"Is the Buick yours?" His voice tried to slice through her unnatural state. What was the matter with her? Lacy asked herself. What was happening? She had never felt anything like this before.

"No, it's my sister's," Lacy replied distantly.

Sloan glanced down at her with some amusement. She looked stunned, otherworldly. He had felt the spark when they touched as well, but he was surprised at the intensity of her reaction. The need to find out what would occur upon further contact drove him on.

As soon as he had put the little dog to rest on the

back seat, he turned to Lacy. Yet he said nothing.
There didn't seem to be a need for verbal expression.
Their eyes said it all. He could read the thoughts in
hers, the unconscious wonder. His mirrored his growing need for discovery.

"Get in," he directed huskily. "I'm coming with
you."

On the only sane level of emotion that remained in
Lacy's brain she knew she should stop everything right
then. She knew she should refuse. She knew she
should make some form of protest. But she did nothing
of the kind. She slid onto the long bench seat and
passed behind the wheel without comment.

Her heart was thundering in her breast and her body
was alive with charged emotion. When he dropped
onto the seat next to her, his hard thigh touching hers,
his hip and shoulder pressed against her, Lacy wanted
to cry out her fear and pleasure. But again, she made no
sound and kept the sensual thrill inside herself.

As the engine came to life, its vibrations only copied
Lacy's energized blood. Was she insane? Was she
crazy? Had there been some kind of debilitating gas let
loose in the air?

Sloan drove the car slowly, a little of Lacy's feeling
of unreality spreading to him. Was he actually here in
her car? Had he almost forced her to get in? And
where was he taking her? All that he knew was that he
wanted to get away from prying eyes, eyes that knew
about him and Caroline. No! Caroline had no part in
this. He wasn't going to think about her. She didn't
own him, at least not yet. He was still free to do as he
pleased with whom he pleased. There had been no
words of total commitment.

Lacy's breathing was becoming more difficult with each second that passed. She *was* crazy. She *was* insane. She should order him to stop. Where were they going?

Sloan depressed the accelerator a little harder as they turned onto the roadway that led out of the exclusive subdivision. Then as soon as that road met the highway he directed their course away from the city and set the car at an even faster pace.

Lacy's dream world seemed to be expanding. She saw the rugged land that flashed by, saw the rolling hills, the scraggly trees that lack of water had stunted in their formative years of growth. Then the car was turning and they were on a narrow, unsurfaced road that seemed to lead nowhere. Soon they stopped under the fragmented shade of a mesquite that was within sight of the very blue water of a distant lake.

The silence was loud after the engine was cut. It practically roared in Sloan's ears. Why did he suddenly feel like an inexperienced fifteen-year-old boy? Afraid to move, afraid to breathe. Then he became aware of Lacy's shuddering intake of breath, and it was as if a flood-filled dam burst its restraining supports. He knew what he wanted—what he had to have!

Lacy was trembling as Sloan turned suddenly to look at her, the message in his eyes one she had never seen before. But instinct told her exactly what it said. For a split second she thought of Richard, then he disappeared under the blaze of blue eyes. When Sloan's arms came out to enfold her and his mouth—that sensual, almost beautiful mouth—came down to touch hers, she lost all capacity to remember anything.

His lips were soft and warm and felt so good. She was aware only of the present, of the feeling that was caus-

ing her to melt against his lean, strong body. Of the
body itself, that burned and breathed and held magic.
Then the kiss began to deepen, his hands on her back
running over the softness of the dress that covered her
flesh while at the same time straining her ever closer.
Lacy's breasts were branding themselves against him.

All coherent thought disappeared from Sloan's mind
as his senses responded independently to her slender
form. He was conscious only of her delicacy, of the
heated softness of her skin through her clothing, of
the sweet fresh taste of her. Lacy's fingers twined in
the golden texture of his hair, feeling the smoothness
of each strand, before moving to trail his neck and outline the working muscles of his back and shoulders.

Then Sloan's lips broke away, but only to pass over
her cheek on a journey to her throat and neck. His
breathing was ragged as he murmured her name. She
gave a soft moan and arched her back. That sign was all
Sloan needed. He pushed her away from him and followed as she came to rest against the well-padded material of the seat.

For timeless seconds Lacy looked up into his vivid
gaze. Never before had she felt such an intense sexual
longing. In fact she had never thought herself capable
of feeling such desire. During her younger years, when
other girls had been experimenting, she had been
either at home studying or in libraries. Sometimes she
didn't know whether it had been her quiet studious nature or the fact that she wasn't particularly a teenage
beauty that had started her off on the road to a more
solitary life, until she actually preferred learning to dat-
ing. That was, until Richard. And with him the entire
relationship had developed along a different plane. At

first he had been the teacher and she the student, then they had been teacher and aid, and, lastly, it had been the blending of two minds rather than two bodies, which she had thought to be the ultimate two humans could achieve in affinity. But now she was being transformed into a student again and she was learning that she had to rethink her naive hypothesis. In fact her supposition was being shattered as if it consisted of nothing more substantial than the thinnest piece of the most fragile crystal.

The weight of Sloan's body entrapped Lacy and she was a willing victim. Not one sound passed her lips as the fire in his gaze flared openly. He lowered his mouth, the white-hot heat of his need sweeping her into a realm she had never entered before. She was burningly aware of him, only of him. When his free hand began to fumble at the buttons of her bodice, she moved so that he could have easier access. Not once did the thought come that they were strangers. That neither knew more than just the basic facts about the other. What they were doing was right!

A muted noise barely penetrated Lacy's consciousness. At first she couldn't identify it. Sloan had freed the opening of her bodice and his head was buried in its folds, his lips on the curve of one breast, his tongue smoothing a liquid trail of arousal throughout her body as it traced the delicate line of her bra edging. His hand had risen to dispense with the hindrance to further pleasure when the sound came again. This time he heard it, too, and his fingers paused, remaining where they were, between the soft material and her sensitized flesh.

The dog barked for a third time. There was a question in his tone and a hint of fear. He had awakened from the sleep he had fallen into during the drive, and he now thought he was alone.

Lacy lay still, extremely conscious of the near melding of their bodies, of the intimate touch of his fingers against her naked skin, of the heat that was generated between them. Her eyes were a molten shade of gold, the yellow slashes seeming to have spread and intensified.

Sloan's fingertips were frozen at her breast, his body aware of her beneath him as he had never been aware of a woman before. Every atom within him seemed to be crying out an impression of her softness, of his driving need. He wanted to tear the clothing from both of their frames and bury himself deep within her, lose himself in her essence, blend their souls in an orgy of physical communion until there was no thought of turning back, no possibility of a presence to interrupt them, no rational sense of care, because they would have already crossed the bridge that led to pure sensation.

Yet when the frightened animal on the rear seat began to whimper, neither of them could ignore his call, and the spell that had carried them in its magic arms released its hold to let reality return them to its firm, exacting grasp.

Sloan's hand moved away reluctantly, and he slowly straightened into his seat just as Lacy resumed her upward position. To keep from looking at her, Sloan turned to reassure the poodle.

"It's OK, boy. We're here." Was that his voice? It was hoarse and tight sounding.

The dog carefully wagged its tail and then rested his

head on his front paws, content to rest once again after finding that he was with friends.

Lacy heard Sloan's husky voice talking to Sampson. She knew what he was doing and she was grateful. Some caretaker she had been to the dog. First he had almost broken his leg, then she had completely forgotten his existence when something much more interesting had arrived to catch her fancy.

Her hands trembled as she started to rebutton her bodice. Why was she thinking such prosaic thoughts? Was it to keep her mind from what had happened? Her fingers slipped. God! What had happened? A sudden rush of emotion engulfed her. She remembered the feel of his lean hard body against her, the straining of his muscles, the heat that emanated from his skin, the way it had felt to be kissed by him, touched by him. She tried again to secure the last button, but her trembling increased so that she couldn't fit the tiny fastening through the allotted hole. She started when long, sensitive fingers took the job away from her.

Her eyes watched his movements, then rose to his face. Was he as shaken as she?

Sloan met the mysterious, yet questioning, gaze. His heart was still thundering in his chest, and it was all he could do not to take her back into his arms. But this time he fought against the urge. He wasn't being fair to her. He wasn't being fair to himself. Not to mention Caroline. An image of a cherub-faced blonde fought its way to the forefront of his mind.

Caroline Stanton had been a part of his life for most of his life. First she had been a towheaded little brat who had dogged his every step as he went about his assigned duties in her father's veterinary office, when he began working there part time in the sixth grade. Then she had become a friend, sharing his enthusiasm for helping animals, and finally she had become more than that. And even though the words had not been said, it was taken for granted that they would marry. It was so right.

"Would it do any good if I said I was sorry?" he questioned gruffly.

Lacy's heart jumped even while it still managed to pound. He was apologizing? Did that mean he regretted what had happened? She looked away as a mass of contradictory feelings greeted that idea. She was all topsy-turvy inside, but still very much aware that she had enjoyed what passed between them. Nothing like that had ever happened to her before. But if he was regretting it...

She held on to some pride by responding, "It's a little late for that, don't you think?" She was relieved to hear how cool she sounded.

Sloan's hands went to the steering wheel and closed on the hard surface. Damn, why did he feel such a heel?

"Maybe," he conceded tightly.

Lacy directed her vision to the arid land ahead of them and to the arm of the highland lake that looked like some kind of azure jewel set in a limestone mount.

"I'll take you back," she heard him say at last, but she made no reply. She couldn't. She didn't trust herself to speak.

The return drive to the subdivision was made in complete silence and Lacy was glad that the trip did not last long. She wasn't sure how much longer she was going to be able to hold on to her control. So many things had happened, so many things she was unaccustomed to dealing with. Never had she allowed herself such uninhibited response. Certainly nothing like that had ever happened with Richard. Oh, there had been touches. He had put his arm around her when they talked in the lab, he had kissed her on the cheek several times. But each occurrence had been so gentle, showing such genuine friendship. They had made her feel all warm inside; she had basked in his approval, knowing that he cared deeply for her and she for him. But this! Lacy stilled the trembling that once again threatened to overcome her body.

Sloan glanced at her from the side of his eye and regretted that he had come to the office that day. He had known it would be a mistake, known that he shouldn't listen to the voice that seemed to impel him to disregard his better judgment. But the pull had been strong, irresistible. And now the mistake had been complicated beyond repair. What had gotten into him? Couldn't he control himself? What was he, an animal?

His jaws tightened. No, that was unfair to all the species he spent his life trying to help. If they acted in a way contradictory to civilized man's refined expectations, it was only because they were programmed to do so. They knew no better. But he did.

Shame made Sloan burn with cold anger, but his irritation was addressed solely to himself. Yet when he spoke, to Lacy's perception, the harshness she sensed radiating from his stiffened form was directed entirely at her, and she responded in kind.

"Where do you live? I'll take you there."

"Don't bother. Anyway, it's my car."

"I said I'd take you home and I will."

"And I'm telling you that I don't want you to!"

Arctic-blue eyes left the paved street ahead to fasten onto her, some of his disgust spilling over because of her stubborn answer.

"Does that chip ever get heavy?"

"Chip?"

"The one I told you about that's on your shoulder."

Lacy's eyes flashed. He was back to being hateful! But in some strange way, she preferred him that way, because at least then she knew better how to deal with him.

"It's not any bigger than your head!"

Sloan was forced to swivel his attention back to the path they were traveling when a car's horn suddenly blared a warning that the Buick was drifting toward the opposite lane.

"Dammit!" Sloan bit out as he quickly righted the car's course, his jaws clamping shut and then grinding, the result of the variety of emotions he was experiencing. It felt good to curse. If it were possible he would vent the entire range of his vocabulary. He would turn the air blue all around him. But he held onto his tongue. The situation was bad enough already.

For some reason Lacy wanted to giggle. She was still smarting from his anger and from the upheaval of spirit she had experienced earlier, but the current situation and his response to it was funny to her. Maybe she was near hysteria. Maybe it was just that she was enjoying his discomfiture. She was trying to control a smile when his glance came back to center on her. To say he was displeased would be a major misrepresentation of the truth. Was it possible for a human being to snarl?

Lacy decided to change tactics. What she wanted

most was to get away from him, to be by herself, to try
to make sense of what had happened. She gave him her
address.

Sloan accelerated immediately. He was torn in different directions. He wanted equally to strangle her for
laughing at him and to kiss her until there was no room
for amusement, until she wanted him as badly as he
still wanted her.

Ariel's home was located without difficulty and the
Buick took the turn into the driveway smoothly. If the
chassis rocked a little at the quick application of brakes,
neither of the occupants seemed to notice. Both opened
their doors simultaneously and glared at each other over
the car's roof.

Remembering an earlier parting the two had en-
dured, Lacy remarked, "Well, I suppose I could say
that that was a fun ride—but I won't." She was proud
of herself for what she considered a nice touch of spite.

Her congratulations soon turned to bitter ashes,
though, when he responded, "No, I agree. The ride
wasn't exactly the high point."

Her features took on an annoyed cast as she spat
back defensively, "I didn't enjoy anything else about it
either!"

Sloan's well-drawn mouth angled into a smile as all
evidence of his previous irritation abated. He still
wasn't pleased with his behavior, but when she looked
at him with those big hazel eyes and almost dared him
to comment, he couldn't resist.

"Would you like for me to show you that you're lying through your teeth?"

Lacy drew a sudden breath. She hadn't expected him
to say that. And from the look of devilish delight in his

blue eyes, he probably would too—right out here in front of everyone.

Lacy collected herself enough to give him a freezing look, her gaze running from his golden hair, looking even lighter in the bright midday sun, down the length of his body that the car did not block. If venom could be transmitted by telepathy, he would be dead.

"No, that won't be necessary." She dismissed his previous question, then to show her disregard, she slammed her door shut and turned, taking time to walk regally down the path to the entryway.

She was almost to the small portico when his odious voice called after her. "Hey—Lacy!"

She froze for an instant. She was undecided about turning around. She was almost to her sanctuary.

"I think you forgot something!"

She checked that her purse strap was firmly planted on her shoulder. That had been her first instinct, would be most women's first instinct. She turned with some confusion, only to be washed again with embarrassment. Sampson! She had left the poor little thing on the backseat. Was she that befuddled? Yes, it seemed she was.

She wasn't about to let her feelings show, though, and when Sloan walked slowly up the path to her, carrying the poodle carefully in his arms, she met his gaze resolutely. She then extended her own arms for a transfer of possession.

As his skin skimmed hers Sloan felt another shaft of desire, a powerful fireball that raced through his frame to center in his loins.

Lacy saw the flame that licked into sudden life in his eyes, and she looked away quickly when her own body began to betray her. Her heart's speed had increased, her breathing was shortened, and a warmth that had nothing to do with the heat of the day came to plague her. She swallowed tightly. She wanted to turn and run, but her legs seemed an extension of the earth.

Then Sampson again came to her rescue. He wiggled until he could reach up to rake the underside of her chin with his soft pink tongue, forgiving her all, while at the same time giving her the opportunity to break away. She mumbled words that could be taken for thanks, then escaped into the safety of the house.

Sloan remained still for several long moments, his gaze riveted on the door. Then he turned and slowly began to make his way along the several mile route that would eventually lead him to the office.

Chapter Five

Lacy was haunted by ghosts that night. Ghosts of the past and of the present. Specters that refused to be exorcized until the glow of the early morning sun fought its way between a gap in the curtain of her bedroom window and chased the night time inkiness away.

She came to groggy awareness and groaned when she realized it was morning. What a night! She had tossed and turned. She would have been better off watching television. Ariel and David had a wide selection of recent movies she could have run on their video recorder. She probably would have been more rested. But she had chosen sleep.

And a lot of good that had done her. Lacy buried her head under her pillow, trying to block out the glare the gap in the curtain was letting in. But in the end she gave up that method. It was too much like being enclosed in a small space, and she had never been comfortable with an experience like that.

She rolled onto her back and stared up at the ceiling as the memory of her dreams came back in vivid technicolor. What need did she have of outside theatrical productions? She made up her own and starred in

them, along with Richard and Sampson and a vet
named Sloan Adams.

Lacy sat forward with a jerk. No! She wasn't going to
let him take hold of her mind so early. Not when she
had lived with him for most of the night.

At her quick movement Sampson stirred on the
cushion that had been placed on the carpet at her bedside. He hadn't liked sleeping alone in the master bedroom, so Lacy had moved him in with her. And since
the accident she was glad that she had.

He gave a wide yawn, his pink tongue curling con-
tentedly out and up like a long, narrow leaf. The sound
he gave as he did this made Lacy smile. At least *he*
seemed to have had a good night, and when he stood to
stretch stiffly and then walk a few paces, she thought
she could detect a little less tentativeness about his gait
than he had exhibited the previous morning.

Her smile increased when the little dog made his way
over to greet her as well as the new day. He still didn't
try to jump on the bed, but his tail wagged with more
enthusiasm. She gathered him to a position beside her
on the covers, suffering a bevy of wet dog-kisses for
her trouble. His hair was like soft silver silk to her sensitive fingers as she stroked him. Soon he lay down, his
button black eyes resting on her face for a few moments before he drifted back into sleep.

Lacy gently touched the tuft of hair that grew on top
of his head. She supposed she would have to contact
her sister today. Yesterday afternoon she had shied
away from the idea because from the degree of upset
she knew she would be unable to hide, Ariel would
only panic and think the poodle's accident was the
cause of her uneasiness. Lacy knew it was not, but

could she ever convince Ariel? And did she want to try to explain? No. If she had done anything right yesterday, it was her decision to put off calling Ariel for another day.

Almost automatically her thoughts turned back to the person who had occupied her unconscious mind for most of the hours of darkness. She remembered everything—the fact and the fiction—and her cheeks flushed at the conclusion of one of her dreams.

Then an echo of Richard's reassuring voice cut through her unease, and she felt a pang of guilt. She had been disloyal to him. He had meant so much to her, and she had repaid his memory with what? A base physical reaction with a man she was much more comfortable disliking than liking?

Lacy clung to the intellectual plane. If she could just forget about Sloan for a time. She concentrated on the project she and Richard had been working on just before he died, one that had fascinated them both, but also one into which they had only just begun to delve. It was complicated and filled with difficulties. If she could only occupy her thoughts with the intricacies involved.

Lacy gave a quiet groan. It was no use. With Richard no longer there to share discoveries, and with a certain doctor of veterinary medicine waiting in the wings to trap any unintentional slip of consciousness, she couldn't maintain her concentration.

She slid from the bed, careful not to disturb the sleeping dog, and padded into the bathroom. Maybe a shower would help lighten her affliction.

Ten minutes later Lacy emerged to find that she wasn't in any better frame of mind than when she started. If anything she was in a worse state. The dream that had given her the most trouble in the early morning hours kept recurring in her waking state. In it she was bathing in a beautiful lagoon on a Pacific atoll, and Sloan had magically appeared beside her in the water. He had smiled at her, his eyes a reflection of the sky above. With natural ease he had begun to kiss her, to caress her. They had ended up lying on the sand, their naked bodies entwined.

Lacy jumped at an imaginary presence as she furiously rubbed a towel over the wetness of her body. It was ridiculous, but it was almost as if she were anticipating Sloan's appearance.

She dressed in a pair of black denims and a cotton pullover shirt and hurried out of the bedroom, hoping that the devils that plagued her could be left there.

She turned on the television, plugged in the percolator, put a piece of bread in the toaster, and, in general, willed herself to the mundane. She ate her breakfast, such as it was, in front of the television, watching a game show that at first she decided was utterly boring and then became involved in. She was still there hours later when the ringing of the telephone finally drew her away.

"Lacy, darling! It's Ariel. I hope I didn't wake you."

"Ariel!" Lacy's heart sank. She wanted to have time to prepare herself, to decide best just how to break the news.

Her sister laughed gaily. "Don't sound so surprised. I'm only in London, not on the moon."

Lacy gave an uneasy laugh herself. Oh, what to say! "No—well, I didn't—"

Ariel interrupted. "Lacy, we've been having so much

fun. Of course David's been in meetings part of the day, and when he is, I shop, but when he's not tied up we've been doing all the tourist things. We saw the palace, Big Ben, some fantastic museums. We even rode the tube. That's their subway, but since I've never been on one of them before, it was truly an experience."

Lacy made a noncommittal reply before her sister continued, her need for breath having been satisfied.

"And, Lacy, I've found you the most adorable dress. It was in this tiny shop—"

Suddenly Ariel stopped, intuition finally having won out over enthusiasm. "What's wrong, Lacy? What's happened? Is it Sampson? Oh, tell me nothing bad has happened to Sampson!"

At the increasing distress in Ariel's tone, Lacy cut in. "No, he's fine. At least he is now. He did get hurt, but—"

"He was hurt! Should I come back? Oh, Lacy, if he needs me—"

"No. Absolutely not. Like I said, he's fine now. A little sore—"

"What happened?"

Lacy took a breath. "He popped his hip out of joint. We were outside, I was watering, and when we came in he ran across the kitchen floor and slipped. He bumped"—she used the gentlest word she could find to describe the jolt the dog had taken—"into a chair leg and his hip slipped out."

"Oh, my God!"

"I took him to an emergency clinic, because it happened on Sunday and the vet there treated him excellently."

"You took him to a strange vet?"

Lacy sighed. "I had to, Ariel. It was either that or let him suffer."

"Suffer!"

"Well, hurt," she qualified.

She heard her sister's sniff come across the ocean. "My poor baby!" she choked.

"I brought him to Dr. Dalton yesterday, and he said he was fine. He's just going to be a little sore. The—the vet I took him to first was there, too."

A silence met those words. Then her sister asked, "What was his name? Was he one of Dr. Dalton's partners?"

Lacy swallowed. "His name is Sloan Adams, and I don't know. All I know is that he was there." Boy, was he there!

"Sloan—Dr. Adams. Oh, I know him."

"You do?"

"Of course. When Dr. Dalton is on vacation or something, Dr. Adams and Dr. Stanton are the only other people I'd trust with Sampson. They're Dr. Dalton's partners and all of them are the very best. They operate the veterinary hospital in our subdivision and one somewhere in Austin itself."

Lacy knew the location well, but she kept that bit of information to herself.

"And you say Sampson is better?" Ariel asked.

Lacy reassured her. "Much. I don't believe he's going to stay sore for as long as we thought. He moved a lot easier this morning. Right now, he's asleep on my bed. When I hang up I'm going to wake him. He probably needs a little time outside."

At that imparted act of normalcy Ariel seemed to calm. "He can walk?"

Lacy gave an understanding smile. "Of course he can walk. He didn't break anything. He's just like his regular self, only a little on the tender side."

The deep concern that had been in her sister's voice on learning of the accident lightened even more. "And he's eating?"

"Everything in sight."

Ariel laughed. It wasn't quite as carefree as her first laugh, but it was definitely beginning to be tinged with happiness again. "He always did like to mooch."

Lacy retained her smile but said nothing.

"Well, I suppose I'd better let you go. We're moving on to Paris tomorrow morning. You do still have the telephone number of the hotel where we'll be staying?"

The list was on the kitchen counter. "Yes."

"And you will let me know if Sampson has any more trouble. You'll let me know immediately?"

"Yes."

A sudden thought struck Ariel. "Why didn't you tell me about this sooner? Were you afraid I'd blame you?"

Lacy's hand tightened on the receiver. "No, not really." At first she had been apprehensive, but later that particular anxiety had been nudged from her mind when it was replaced by another.

"Listen, Lacy." Ariel became serious. "Sampson means a lot to me. You know he does. And I'd be heart-broken if anything really serious ever happened to him, but you mean so much more. You're my sister. I want what's best for you. Don't ever be afraid to come to me with a problem. That's what a big sister is for."

A haze of tears surfaced in Lacy's hazel eyes. If only she could tell Ariel!

"Now I really must get off before we owe the telephone company something equal to the national debt. Take care, Lacy. And remember, call me if you need me."

"I will," she promised.

When her sister was gone, Lacy placed the receiver back onto its wall mount before slowly turning to make her way back to her bedroom.

Sloan awakened Tuesday morning with a blinding headache. It had been a stupid thing to do. Drink had never agreed with him. Other men could down one beer after another and never be fazed. But not he. After two he quietly slipped into a deep, dreamless sleep, and then the next day woke up wishing he had never been born—or at the very least, that he had been born smarter. That was why he seldom drank anything at all. He knew his intolerance and stayed away. But yesterday had been such a rotten day. Maybe, unconsciously, he had wanted to be punished for his actions. So what better way than a hangover?

He ran a hand over the golden stubble on his chin and peered into the bathroom mirror with bloodshot eyes. What a wonderful specimen *you* are, he thought. Some macho man. He gave a short laugh, then grimaced as an equally short pain jolted through his head.

The hot water coming from the shower helped somewhat, yet nothing but a little time was going to make a real difference. Still, he lingered under the spray, letting the stinging droplets drive into his upper back and neck, then his chest, and once again his back, while steam rose in billowing clouds to fill the entire room.

Sloan dried himself briskly with a fluffy yellow towel,

then hitched it around his narrow hips. He approached the mirror again and after removing the steamy film from its surface, lathered his face in preparation for his shave.

He wished he didn't have to go into the office today. He could just imagine what would happen to his head if one of the dogs brought in for his care barked loudly. But stupidity always exacted a price, and his duty would be to serve while not feeling the best in the world.

After shaving away all traces of the golden beard that attempted the same amount of growth each night, he splashed water on his face, dried it, then applied a spicy cologne.

Following that, he once more inspected himself in the mirror. Well, that was a little better. He still wouldn't win any prizes, but at least now he looked as if he might live. Sloan dropped the towel and moved into his bedroom. He dressed in a pair of corded navy jeans and a white Ocean Pacific T-shirt.

At the idea of breakfast, he shuddered. Lord, no way! Maybe he could stomach a cup of coffee later, but right now he didn't want to face even that.

He slipped his thin-line wallet into his back pocket and pulled on his watch. He was a few minutes early. He moved over to the long, narrow set of windows that overlooked the magnificent view of a rocky hillside, and stood just inside the parted curtain. The light stabbed at his eyes, but after blinking several times, he could stand it.

What was *she* doing this morning? the idle thought jumped into his mind. Lacy. He repeated the name just under his breath, and a vision of her as he had last seen her, standing before him with her eyes flashing both resentment and embarrassment, caused his body to give the sensual response he was beginning to expect whenever he was near her or even thought of her.

And as he remembered more—the heady feel of her soft, pliant body in his arms, the warm responsiveness of her lips, the ultra-creamy smoothness of her skin where the beautiful curves of her breasts began—the erotic sensation increased until it became an actual pain.

How he wanted her!

Sloan gave an agonized groan and moved away from the window, letting the curtains fall back into place. In the dimness of the room he stumbled to the bed and rested on its edge.

His head had started a repetition of its previous pounding and a thin outbreak of perspiration was covering his forehead and the area above his upper lip. As he wiped the wetness away, a momentary feeling of helplessness warred with rage at the fates for allowing this to happen to him.

Why couldn't he control himself, control his feelings? Why did this one woman—a stranger, practically—have such a strong pull on him? Why she and not Caroline? Why couldn't it be Caroline? She was the woman he had thought to be his soul mate.

But as nicely put together as Caroline's body was, she had never made him burn as if he was suddenly struck by a fever, had never consumed him to the point of making him forget all else. Yet he loved her. And that was what made all of this so hard to understand. She was his friend, the closest friend he possessed. And yet...

Didn't the years and degree of caring count for anything? Sloan gritted his teeth and set his jaw firmly. He could get over this, this temporary insanity. Never again was he going to allow himself to be put in the position he had been in yesterday.

When he had returned to the office after completing his long walk, Mrs. Steinbeck, the receptionist, had given him one of her pinched looks of disapproval. And for such a boisterous, assertive personality, Max had tiptoed around the cause of his disappearance, telling him in a confidential tone that Caroline had called, looking for him.

Damn it all! Sloan swore. He was an honorable man. He didn't enjoy not being comfortable with himself or with having other people think badly of him. He wasn't the kind of person who chased every skirt that swished in his direction. In the past the number of women he had had opportunity to dally with far outnumbered the ones he had actually developed a relationship with.

And now, at thirty-one, he had thought he was close to settling down. The idea of a wife and family was beginning to appeal; the instinct for closeness was upon him.

He had worked hard all his life, his father having just walked out of their home one day never to come back. When his mother's paycheck barely stretched to cover food and clothing, he had taken a job in Jim Stanton's veterinary clinic. And from that moment his life had taken form.

The debt he owed Jim caused Sloan's conscience to sink. Because how was he repaying him? By betraying his daughter? No! He couldn't do that. Jim had kept him employed all through high school, teaching him, sharing with him, shaping him. Jim had even paid the expenses that his scholarship at the university didn't cover. He had made his entire professional life possible.

What Sloan felt for Lacy was purely and simply lust. He had experienced it before in lesser degrees. He recognized the signs. Love was friendship, a growing friendship.

Sloan pushed restlessly to his feet and at the same moment glanced again at his watch.

Great! Now he was late. It was a good thing he wasn't going to have to drive into Austin to work at the clinic. As was his usual habit, Jim was covering it alone today, while Max and he took care of the office in the suburbs.

Sloan ran a hand over his neck as if the muscles were already tired from having to hold up his head.

In the beginning he had thought that renting this apartment in the exclusive subdivision where the new second office was located was a viable idea. Jim had encouraged him, saying that one of them should live close by. And since Sloan was the only partner not married and was capable of pulling up his roots without much trouble, he had agreed. Now, he wasn't so sure about his decision.

By the time Sloan broke for lunch he felt exhausted. His fears about the barking dogs had been realized. Every animal for miles around that specialized in loud, sharp yaps must have decided that today was his day for an appointment.

Sloan thanked God there was no midday surgery scheduled. With the mood he was in he wouldn't want to inflict himself on some poor helpless animal.

He was just taking his lab coat off and hanging it on a peg when warm, soft hands came up to cover his eyes.

"I'll give you one guess," a husky feminine voice warned.

Sloan's heart jumped, but not because of Caroline's nearness. It leaped from the after-effects of a guilty conscience.

"Then I guess I'll have to be right." He pretended to think, but in reality he was conquering his unease. The hands released their hold and he slowly turned around, forcing a crooked smile. "Caroline—"

A blond head sporting a mass of fluffy curled hair tilted to one side. "Sure, you say that now."

"I knew who you were all along."

"Uh-huh! I bet!" She pretended disbelief but began to grin, the smile lighting a rounded face with a bow-shaped mouth and a nose that was definitely pug. Caroline had the kind of looks that went perfectly with turn-of-the-century clothing, upswept hairdos, and big floppy hats loaded with tons of millinery tulle and flowers. The rest of her body agreed with her face. She had an almost hourglass figure that required a series of diets to keep it from becoming overblown. Today she was dressed in a very modern skirt and blouse.

Sloan kept his smile firmly in place, and Caroline reached out to collect his arm as she turned to the door. "You know, sometimes you're a hard man to find. Ever since you came back from Boston, you've been so busy. I tried to call you yesterday. Max said you'd been here, but—"

Sloan cut in. "I've had some things to take care of."

Caroline waved to Mrs. Steinbeck, who was listening uninhibitedly, and Sloan glanced heavenward. Why to-

day of all days? He wished he could have just called
Caroline tonight and dealt with everything tomorrow.
Then the traitorous feeling that thought produced
made him feel even worse.

They had reached the outer door when Caroline
laughingly teased, "There's only one way you can re-
deem yourself, Dr. Adams. You can take me to lunch.
Tina is minding the studio, so we have at least an
hour."

Sloan reached out to turn the knob. "Sounds good."

Caroline reached up to pat his cheek. "I thought so,
too. I've seen so little of you, I decided to kidnap you if
I had to."

Sloan opened the door and Caroline walked through.
But before he moved outside himself, he glanced back
at Mrs. Steinbeck. A deeper look of disapproval was
now darkening her brow than had been there the previous day. When he frowned, she looked away.

Lunch with Caroline was a further ordeal. Sloan listened as best he could while she chatted happily about
her business of selling the handcrafted articles of various local artists. He even made humorous observa-
tions, although where they came from only the gods
knew. He was determined to make up to Caroline for
his lapse.

"Alicia says my range of displays is much superior to
those at The Pink Cactus." She named a competing
studio that had recently opened.

Sloan searched his memory. "Alicia?"

Caroline nodded, her blond curls bouncing. "Alicia
Harrison. You met her at that dinner the Art Commis-
sion gave last spring. She's backed a number of artists

in the area, made it possible for some of them not to have to worry about where their next meal is coming from, so they can devote themselves to their work.''

When Sloan just continued to look at her, Caroline giggled, "I can see she made a big impression on you."

Sloan blinked, then a smile came into his eyes. "Yeah, I guess she did." He finished the Coke that had accompanied their pasta.

For the next few minutes all was silent between them. Then Caroline pushed her plate away. "That was delicious."

Sloan said nothing, continuing his study of the tablecloth. He felt her eyes examine him, but he didn't lift his gaze.

Finally she sighed, "I know this isn't the right time, Sloan, not when we're both almost staggering with lasagna, but you are coming to dinner tomorrow night, aren't you? I know you couldn't make it last week; you were too tired from the trip, but—"

As the sentence was left to hang in the air, Sloan felt an unseen noose begin to tighten. Mentally he tried to strain against it, but in the end he relented. "Sure I'll be there. What time?"

Caroline frowned slightly. "Why, the usual, of course."

Sloan nodded, while all the time calling himself an idiot. He had only been going over to the Stantons' for Wednesday night dinner as long as he could remember!

He made a show of rubbing his temple and gave the excuse, "Sorry. I'm a little muzzy."

Immediately Caroline was all concern. "I thought something was wrong." She leaned forward to place her palm against his forehead for a testing second. "You aren't coming down with anything, are you? Something you picked up in Boston?"

If the situation had been a farce, Sloan would have laughed. What a play on words: *Something he had picked up in Boston.* Could Lacy be labeled that? The smile he gave was ironic. "No, I don't think so. It's just a head-ache."

"Have you taken anything for it?"

"A couple of aspirin. What I needed most was food."

Caroline loked at his still half-filled plate. "Well, you certainly didn't eat very much."

A rush of irritability made Sloan want to tell her to mind her own business. Yet he kept his tongue and said instead, "I had all I wanted." He hadn't had the heart to refuse her desire for Italian food, but consideration of his uneasy stomach would have made his choice something different.

"You really don't look very well."

"I'll be fine. Don't fuss."

Caroline giggled again. "We sound like an old married couple."

A pang of disquiet shot through Sloan. "Maybe we just know each other too well."

Caroline was silent, deep in thought. Then she shrugged her shoulders and stood up to leave. "Do you want me to call you tomorrow to remind you about dinner?"

Sloan came to an upright position as well. "No, I'll remember," he answered quietly.

"Are you sure? You're becoming as forgetful as my father."

"I'm sure." At that moment Sloan might have promised her anything. He had to get away. Everything was beginning to crush him. He needed some time to be by himself. He took her arm and after paying the bill, accompanied her to the car.

For the next week Sloan tried to keep his attention firmly attached to the necessities of a doctor's life. He tended his patients, operated when called on, calmed his patients' owners' fears, gave the necessary inoculations and examinations, and took his turn manning the emergency night clinic.

He even went over to the Stantons' for Wednesday night dinner, where he was able to keep the conversation directed primarily to things veterinary. But as minds so often do, his seemed to have a will of its own, and at odd times, when he was least resistant to intrusion, thoughts of Lacy rose up to accost him.

By Monday night he could stand it no longer. Caroline was visiting a friend who was ill, Jim was on duty, and he—he was restless. He decided to get into his car and drive. He didn't care where. He just had to go somewhere, do something.

Lacy spent the first few days of the week in a state of agitated misery, mainly because she was unnerved and ashamed about what had happened. She wasn't the kind of woman to allow such intimacies at the drop of a hat, or rather, at the drop of a pair of pants. At least she hadn't thought she was. And yet she couldn't expel Sloan Adams or his ability to stir her from her memory. Disgustedly she resolved that it would be wonderful if uncomfortable people and occurrences could be erased as easily as a teacher erased a blackboard.

But what made the situation even worse was that lately whenever she tried to conjure a comforting vision of Richard, it wouldn't come. It was as if he had been made up of particles of smoke, and the greater the number of days since his passing, the more obscure his image became. The first time it had happened, she had panicked. She needed his protection. Then, as successive attempts failed to produce a desired result, she swallowed her fear and tried to bury herself in her sister's library. Books had always been her salvation; they would be once again. But this time even her usual deliverance let her down. Her taste and her sister's taste were in direct contrast. The multitude of paperback romances that took up almost every bookshelf couldn't possibly keep her enthralled. Or maybe she didn't want to become enthralled. Lacy thumbed through one or two and found that each seemed to try to outdo the other in how fast and how often the main characters could be thrown together in a clinch—or worse.

Almost in desperation Lacy drove into Austin proper that afternoon and visited the University library. There, in familiar surroundings, she found a wealth of information that did appeal to her.

She loved her work, found it fascinating. Genetic research had so many applications. The area she had been involved in, preparing and testing vaccines for their ability to eliminate infection, was still her first love. But all new discoveries in the field were interesting to her. When immersed in an intensive research project, she had little time to keep up with unfolding developments, but now...

After several hours, Lacy reluctantly pushed away from the table, and conscious of the little dog at home, she returned the various journals and periodicals she had gathered. She was sure that during her absence Sampson had been sleeping, but she didn't want to leave him alone for too long.

When she arrived at Ariel's home, she found that what she had suspected was indeed fact; the dog was happy to see her, but the yawns he gave showed that he had not wasted any time pining for her.

Assured in that knowledge Lacy returned to the library for a few hours each afternoon the remainder of the week. Getting out of the house helped her spirits a great deal, but as the newness began to wear off, she once again became conscious of a growing restlessness. And memories of Sloan Adams began to intrude even in the quietness of the library.

By Monday Sampson was well on the road to recovery, the discomfort he had first experienced becoming less and less. He had improved so much that Lacy had no qualms about bathing him that night. Even for an aristocratic poodle he was beginning to smell very much like a dog, especially when he had missed his bath the weekend before because of his injury. Scooping him into her arms she transported him to the kitchen and placed him in the sink. That was the easiest place for the project, Ariel had told her. And with a good scouring afterwards...

When the poodle was thoroughly wet, Lacy couldn't help smiling at the picture he made. He looked like nothing more than a very large rat, except that his eyes were big and woeful and his hair, where he stood in warm water, floated out around his thin little legs in silky billows. Working as quickly as she could she lathered and rinsed him, aware that he was beginning to shake. She didn't know if it was from being too cool—she had turned the air conditioner several degrees higher—or whether he simply didn't like taking baths. She was just wrapping him in a towel, promising him that he was going to be the most handsome dog in the country, when the doorbell rang.

For a moment Lacy ceased all motion, the damp towel, with the dog enclosed, hugged to her breast. Who could it be? She had contacted no one. From the beginning she had decided that she wasn't ready yet to renew old acquaintances. Then she relaxed. She was being silly. It was probably one of Ariel's neighbors wanting to borrow something. Or, possibly, it was a child who had lost his ball across the fence and needed permission to go into the backyard to get it.

Lacy took a dry towel and placed it over Sampson. Whoever it was, she would carry her excuse to get rid of him with her. It would be obvious that she was busy.

When she approached the front door, Lacy shifted her burden so that she could have one hand free. Then she twisted the knob and applied a polite smile of inquiry to her lips.

The smile remained for only one brief second, because the person who stood on the doorstep was no neighbor. He was no child. Instead he was the man she had been trying so hard to eject from her memory. The intruder was Sloan Adams.

Chapter Six

Magnetic blue eyes blazed into her own before sweeping downward to the bundle she held in her arms. When they rose once again, some of the fire had been controlled.

"Am I paying a visit at the wrong time?"

Lacy was astounded first by the man's surprise appearance, and second by his audacity. Paying a visit indeed! She collected her wits, which had been scattered by the thrust of his gaze and returned, "I didn't know vets paid house calls." She adjusted the door so that she could put one knee firmly to the wood. She wasn't about to let him in.

"This vet does."

Lacy was nonplussed for a moment. Then she rallied. "Well, as you can see, Sampson is being well taken care of."

"I didn't come to see the dog."

Again Lacy was temporarily silenced. "Then who—?" The question escaped before she could stop it. If it wasn't the poodle, then it had to be her.

A gold brow arched into a fallen tuft of hair. A warm wind was blowing and had disturbed the smoothly combed style, either that or the man had used his fingers as a comb. But the disarray only added to his appeal, and the muscles in Lacy's legs began an involuntary weakening.

"I came to see you."

The quiet reply made Lacy's enervation complete. It was all she could do to keep upright on her feet.

Sloan looked down into the eyes that seemed to hold a mixture of emotions, dazed shock being the most prominent. He had driven for what had seemed to be hours, but in fact it was probably only one at most. Then he had turned back onto the road that retraced his path to his apartment with every intention of going to bed early if he had to in order to bring an end to this terribly long day. When the turn-in came, though, he silently passed it by. As if having a will of its own, the car drove on. And when he found himself once again in front of the house on Willow Street, he could no more resist the need to see her than a salmon could halt its relentless swim upstream.

Lacy blinked; the rosy glow of the late-setting sun cast its color onto the fluffy white clouds that had gathered in the western sky.

"No." The denial was automatic.

Sloan took a step forward, and forgetting her earlier determination, Lacy took one back, leaving the door unattended. The doctor's arm came out to brace it, and Lacy moved further within. Giving a slow smile, Sloan crossed the threshold.

Lacy didn't know what to do. She wasn't exactly afraid of him, but then again, she was. What did she know of him, really?

She began to bluster. "Look, you can't do this."

Sloan feigned a look around. "I think I already have."

"Well you shouldn't!"

"I shouldn't do a lot of things."

"Get out!"

"No."

Lacy acutely felt her helplessness, and she unconsciously began to hold the poodle as if he were a shield.

Sloan watched her, momentarily unable to think of anything further to say. Again he was forcing a situation, one in which he wasn't even sure he should be involved. It was as if his instincts were compulsively leading him onward—instincts that were bent upon a heedless race across unbroken ground—and when he gave pause, he suddenly became uncertain of where to place his next step.

His gaze glided over Lacy's features, taking in the soft, clean lines of her cheek and jaw, the slightly tipped nose, the beautifully formed curve of her mouth, which he knew could be warm and responsive. His attention rose, and he examined the way the fine hairs growing on her brow arched like twin butterfly wings ready to take delicate flight, the way the dark ring of her lashes brought out the yellowish-brown color of her eyes. Then he saw something else. Like a skittish fawn startled by her first scent of man, she was wary of him. He could read both fear and fascination in her gaze.

That realization quickened his imaginary lagging gait. He motioned easily to the dog. "He needs to be dried."

The soft, gentle voice went a long way toward soothing Lacy's jumping nerves. After a timeless second she was able to tear her eyes away from the captivation of his and glance down at Sampson, who was waiting patiently in her arms.

Buttons of jet-black gazed up at her, the towel having slipped away from covering his head. A tentative sound came from the silvered throat as dampened curls poked up on his head. One convulsive tremble was soon followed by another. Lacy adjusted the covering and held him closer. Sloan Adams's steady gaze was still on her when she looked up.

"He's chilled," she accused, taking refuge in the first defense she could find. The way he was looking at her unnerved her. It was as if he was in contact with a part of her being that remained a mystery to the rest of the world and sometimes even to herself.

"That's why I said he needed to be dried."

Lacy stared at the man. "Then leave, so that I can!"

"Don't you ever give up?"

A little of the fight Lacy thought had cowardly disappeared as soon as he made entry into the house resurfaced and she retorted smartly, "If you knew me better you wouldn't ask that." Give up were two words that definitely were not a part of a researcher's vocabulary.

"And if you knew me better, you'd know that that's exactly what I'm trying to do."

Lacy frowned. The man was talking in circles.

Sloan's smile slowly increased until it could be termed dazzling. "I want to get to know you better," he enlightened.

That simple answer caused a surge of powerful white-hot flame to shoot through Lacy's bloodstream while memory painted her cheeks a violent crimson.

She turned away to hide her reaction and started to walk into the living room. She couldn't just stand there and have him watch her discomfort. And anyway, as far as she was concerned, they had already learned far too much about each other.

When she turned her back on him, Sloan grimaced. Boy, was he making progress! He followed her into the large room and let his glance move over the modern yet comfortable furnishings before returning to Lacy. She was plugging in a slim, hand-held hair dryer.

"I'm an expert at that. Would you like some help?" He made the offer, but she ignored it.

Sloan tucked his hands into the front pockets of his slacks as she sank to a seat on the couch, uncovered the dog from his wrap, and flipped the switch on the plastic handle, causing the appliance to hum loudly.

Everything would have been perfect for Lacy if Sampson had cooperated. The noise the dryer made covered any words Sloan might say, but, as well, it startled the little dog, who, once he had received some of the freedom he had so patiently been biding his time for, began the struggle to be totally free. For so small an animal the poodle suddenly seemed to have immense strength and determination. It was all Lacy could do to keep him on her lap, mindful that she still had to be careful with him because of his recent injury.

"Sampson—no! Wait! Hold still!"

She might have been talking to feathers, so great an impact did her directives have. The dog continued to wiggle and squirm until two large hands lifted him into the air.

Lacy leaned back against the rear cushion and, with some irritation, clicked the dryer switch off. Her eyes rose to meet Sloan's resentfully. Did he have to interfere in everything?

"It's easier if you do it this way," Sloan confided. Then, easing himself down, he sat on the floor, his legs folded at the knee. "Come on, boy." He flipped the dog onto his side and held out a hand to Lacy for the dryer. Sampson wiggled once or twice, but the hand on his back was the hand of authority and he knew it. When the dryer came to life once again, it was on a lower setting and the dog remained still.

"See? It's not so hard."

Lacy felt bitchy. "I didn't know veterinarians spent their time grooming dogs. I thought they had better things to do."

Sloan's blond head was bent to his task, his long, sensitive fingers running through the silver hair so that the warm air might dry it more efficiently.

"This is something you don't forget."

Lacy shifted position until she was sitting up straight. "What poor dog did you practice on? Your own?"

"I've never owned a dog."

His admission disconcerted her. She frowned slightly. "I thought all animal doctors loved animals."

"You shouldn't make such sweeping assumptions."

"You don't?" Her surprise was evident in her tone.

She sensed Sloan's smile rather than saw it. Then when he glanced up, his eyes an incredible shade of blue in his tanned face, the twinkle that was showing with unabashed enjoyment revealed that he was having fun at her expense.

"You're making another assumption," he said softly.

Lacy stared at him. From almost the first moment they met, he had either been laughing at her or making love to her. At that her thoughts skidded to a halt and she threw him a heated, defensive glare.

"What about you?" Sloan pretended not to notice her aggravation. "Do you have any pets?

"No!"

"Then that accounts for it."

"Accounts for what?"

"Your irritability."

The little bits of yellow came to life in Lacy's hazel eyes. At last. He had given her a perfect opportunity. "Is that your excuse?" she asked sweetly.

Sloan directed the dog's head onto one thigh and began to dry his ears. "I don't need an excuse."

"Then you admit that you're not exactly a knight in shining armor?"

"Do you want one?" His inquisitive gaze made a foray of her features.

Not for the first time Lacy felt as if she were twirling on one of those playground contraptions that was propelled by foot power until it was turning faster than the runner could run; then, exhausted, the child would cling to the curved metal rail while the world flashed giddily by. Did he always have a ready answer?

"This entire conversation is ridiculous. What I want is for you to leave."

"You have beautiful eyes."

"Right now!"

"Are you going to be in Austin long?"

"Am I going to have to call the police?"

"Would you like to have dinner with me?"

Lacy was trembling at the end of that exchange, mostly because of her impotence in being able to budge him. But there was also something else. That same pull, that attraction. There he was, sitting like an Indian in the middle of Ariel's living room floor, Sampson on his lap, with those fantastic blue eyes turned on her, that appealingly handsome face raised, that mane of golden blond hair, with its slightly curling texture, just waiting for her to reach out and slide her fingers through it—all virile American male—and she wanted to throw him out? Even to the extent of forcibly removing him if he wouldn't go voluntarily? A part of her wondered if there was another woman in the entire world who would contemplate such an action. Probably not! she answered her own question. But she wasn't like all the other women in the world. She was herself, Lacy.

Yet as the seconds ticked away on an invisible, silent clock her resolve crumbled, and she found that she wasn't nearly as adamant as she pretended.

"No, I can't—" She tried to bolster her fading resolve and racked her brain for an excuse. "I can't leave Sampson."

Sloan flicked the power switch off, and the room was once more silent.

"He's a dog, you know. Not a child."

"I still can't."

"Can't—or won't?"

Lacy's chin came up. "If you want brutal honesty, then no, I won't."

The doctor let the poodle escape, and Sampson took two steps before pausing to shake himself carefully from the tip of his nose to the end of his fluffy tail. Sloan chuckled at the sight and Lacy's heart jumped. She liked the sound he made when he was enjoying something. Quickly she shook her head. No! She wasn't going to think that way. Not now. Not with him here.

"Would you come for a walk?" He had turned back to her.

Lacy sighed. He was like a sculptor, whittling away at a block of marble bit by bit until he achieved the goal he was determined to find. She met his smiling gaze. He knew what he was doing. And she was afraid that he had almost as accurate an idea of how he was affecting her. Should she continue to fight? So far it hadn't achieved anything. And what harm could come from a walk?

"May Sampson come?"

For the first time since he had entered the house, Sloan's spirits brightened. At last he was making progress. He wanted her to trust him, he wanted her to like him, he wanted her to— He put a brake on his careening thoughts. One step at a time, old man, he told himself. One step at a time.

"Sure. It would probably do him good."

Lacy tried to delve beneath the bright blue twinkle. Was that a flash of triumph she had momentarily seen? That suspicion underscored her previous doubts. Just what did she know of Sloan Adams, other than the fact that he strongly appealed to a side of her that she hadn't exercised before? Wasn't that enough? She began to shake her head in a negative motion.

Sloan was quick to step in. "We won't go far. Just to the park a few blocks away." He paused, then asked softly, "You're not afraid of me, are you?"

Lacy covered her start by rising to her feet. "I'll get his collar and leash." She walked into the kitchen to retrieve the thin leather strap from the counter and the leash from the hook where it hung in the attached utility room, all the while wondering if she was that transparent. And, if she was, didn't she have cause?

Her face was composed as she reentered the living room. He was now on his feet, his entire demeanor one of total calm. Suave and debonair, the words stood out in her mind. She could have been describing an old-time Hollywood film star, only he was definitely not an image on celluloid. He was very much a living, breathing source of sensual masculinity. His brown slacks and short-sleeved tan shirt fitted him perfectly, emphasizing the excellent physical condition of his body.

Lacy walked directly to the dog and attached his collar and lead, while all the time a little voice in her subconscious tried to tell her that she was making a bad mistake. But she couldn't go back on her decision. She would lose face if she did. With him and, more important, with herself.

The walk started out rather staidly: Lacy on one edge of the sidewalk and Sloan on the other, with Sampson ahead of them, pulling excitedly on the leash. Very little conversation passed between the two humans, each seemingly willing to be a part of the silence. Then, gradually, as the warmth of the newly fallen dusk settled peacefully on the surrounding hills and the pools of light the street lamps emitted became friendly guides to each step, beckoning them from one darkened area to the next, an inexplicable contentedness sprang up between them.

Sloan's hands were pushed deeply into his front pockets and his face was turned forward, the profile Lacy had been hesitant to look at more than once, utterly at home, seemingly completely satisfied with life as it was. At that moment he couldn't think of another place he would rather be in the entire world.

Lacy held the looped leather strap between the

curled fingers of her right hand and measured her steps to fall in with his. And no matter how often she told herself that this was crazy, that she should be back in Ariel's living room with the door safely barred, the strange sense of warm comfort his presence provided couldn't be shaken.

"It's nice out tonight." The gentle huskiness of his voice disturbed the air.

"Yes." Lacy agreed, still caught up in the magic of the moment.

Sampson stopped to investigate an interesting smell that clung to a particular spot of grass then hurried onward, not making his companions even pause.

Several more steps were taken before Sloan spoke again. "He looks almost back to normal."

Lacy glanced up at him, only quickly to follow his gaze as it was directed at the dog. "Yes," she agreed again, but some of the contentment she had been experiencing began to evaporate. Why was it that every time she looked at him this nervous knot centered itself exactly in her middle? And why did it spread to include her entire being when he looked back? Was it only sexual awareness? Yes, it was definitely sexual awareness.

Lacy gave a self-conscious cough and raised a hand to cover it. But once she saw the involuntary trembling of her fingers, she knew she had to gain control of herself. She was an intellectual; she should act like one. Only she was suddenly at an impasse as to know how to go about it. Intellectuals begat little intellectuals, didn't they? And they didn't do it through osmosis. They were blessed with the same feelings as other human beings, a fact she was just beginning to appreciate. So what should she do? Relax and enjoy becoming familiar with another form of the learning experience?

At that thought her lips curved into a smile, and the desire to confide her interior joke with Sloan was strong. But sanity prevailed and she controlled the impulse.

Sloan noticed the smile and wondered at its cause, yet, instinctively, he didn't question her, deciding that he just might not like the answer.

Once they crossed into the park, and only the moon and stars lighted their path, a part of Lacy wanted to turn back. Now she could see the danger in a walk. But another part of her wanted to go on, to experience anything that might come, to feel once again the hardness of his body pressed against hers, to taste the honeyed nectar of his kisses. Her wayward side won. Without a word Lacy walked onward, her awareness of Sloan at her side intensifying with each step she took.

That was why, when he stopped and turned to her, she automatically echoed the movement.

The eyes looking up at him were almost hypnotic in their effect on Sloan. It was like being caught up in a storm of pure sensation. The moon was bathing the clear creaminess of her skin, causing it to glow like smooth alabaster; he was breathing the heady sweetness of her short, shallow breaths. Her tongue appeared to glisten her slightly parted lips, and with a soft groan, Sloan could resist the rush of passion no longer. He reached out to cup the sides of her cheeks and bent his head until the moisture on her mouth became a part of his.

The combined feel of his sensitive yet strong fingers

holding her face upward to receive his kiss, and the touch of his lips to hers caused a pleasurable glow to spread its licking molten heat throughout Lacy's body. For several earth-shattering moments her entire life drew its elemental force from that one connection, all sensation deriving from the partial coupling. Then as the kiss began to deepen, Sloan's breaths becoming harsher with his mounting arousal, his tongue beginning a more intimate invasion into the silken recess beyond her responsive lips, and his hands dropping to start a compulsive massaging of her lower back, Lacy suddenly yearned for more. And the irrefutable evidence of the depth of his desire as he pulled her hips firmly to his made her overwhelmingly aware that he was experiencing the same carnal urges as she was.

Lacy allowed her body to melt against his, her heated breasts fusing into his muscular chest, her arms rising to entwine his neck. The leash loop went unheeded as it dropped the length of her upraised arm to rest enclosed at her shoulder. Her fingers were busy, at last stroking the hair that had so long intrigued her. It was the consistency of the softest mink, rich and luxuriant, like touching liquid gold. Then her fingers fell to exploring the warm skin at the back of his neck and the hard, working muscles of his back as he strained her even closer.

As had happened before, primitive necessity asserted itself the instant the two of them touched. And again Lacy was no match for it. Whatever he wanted, she would do. She knew she had only to give the signal and they would stretch onto the coolness of the grass, acting out her fantasy.

Before she could give action to her wanton inclination, though, Sloan was tearing his lips from hers, breaking the union, confusing her by his withdrawal.

She could not see his face in the shadowed darkness, but she could still feel his need, feel the way his body was continuing to respond to hers, feel the burning heat. And when he bent to nuzzle the oversensitized flesh at the base of her neck, she gasped, expecting another onslaught. Yet the hands that were now clasping her arms just above the elbow did not move. Nor did they tighten.

Sloan straightened and gazed down into the moonlit passion written plainly on her face and called himself all kinds of a fool. She was ready. He could take her. She couldn't blame him later for forcing her. But he couldn't do it. He wanted her. How he wanted her! His body was one entire ache, with the most painful area the throbbing phallus that was demanding satisfaction. It would be so easy to forget the consequences and give in to nature's most fascinating and appealing game. Yet, through sheer force of will, he controlled his surging impulses and continued to hold her away.

A tight smile tilted his lips as he suggested huskily, "I think we'd better stop."

When she just continued to stare up at him, her hair in disarray around her shoulders, Sloan knew another moment of intense temptation. But somehow he found the strength. Echoing his earlier half-formed decision, he became determined to raise her opinion of him. He wanted to become more than just someone who could blaze the path to a sexual partnership. He wanted to get to know her, know the way she thought, know every little nuance that made her her. And the idea frightened him. Heaven knew he hadn't planned anything of this sort. He hadn't planned any of it. But the longer he thought about it, the more he wanted it, and he wasn't going to allow anything—anything—to kill that tentative reach for a flowering of understanding between them. Not even himself.

"You're some woman, Lacy," he murmured.

Lacy blinked. Was she standing on the ground? She still had the sensation of floating. She didn't know what to say. Instead she gave a shaky little laugh and returned, "I could say the same for you."

A stray moonbeam illuminated his teasing smile. "Oh, I should hope not."

Lacy swallowed. "That—that's not exactly what I meant."

Sloan chuckled and gave her a momentary hug. "I know," he soothed. "I know." Then he pushed her away and broke the contact of their bodies.

Once she was totally supporting her own weight Lacy took an unsteady step, causing the napping poodle to come to attention. Like all dogs who become bored when their masters decide to involve themselves in something completely human, Sampson had passed his time doing what canines do best—sleeping.

Lacy's gaze flew downward, probing the shadows until she found the silvered form. She had done it again. She had forgotten him. Why was it every time she was in Sloan's company all logical thought flew out the nearest window? Then her eyes slowly traveled the length of the body still standing so close to her own, and she knew why. The reason was the most basic on earth.

Richard! Where are you? The cry reverberated throughout her mind. But the plea went unanswered.

Her memory of him was like a mirage. The more intensely she searched, the more elusive it became. As a result Lacy became frightened. She didn't like what was starting to happen to her. Or rather, maybe she was beginning to like it too much.

As her perusal lifted from slim hips, over flat stomach, to deep masculine chest, another rush of awareness washed over her. And all further effort to resist his attraction was swept away, at least for the time being. She watched as Sloan hunched down to ruffle the tuft of hair that grew on the poodle's head. Then, as he straightened, she quickly looked away.

Sloan's expression was blank while he examined the profile presented to him. Was she pulling away from him again? Closing up? His finger came out to touch her chin and bring it around to face him. As he saw the remaining glow that gave unspoken lie to his fear, he took courage and whispered softly, "Come on. Let's walk."

Lacy followed his direction without giving it a second thought. It was good that they should continue. She didn't want to go home immediately. She wanted the moment to last. The arm he protectively placed about her shoulders seemed, strangely, to belong there.

They spoke very little for the remaining hour it took to circle the park, walk several blocks further, and then turn around to retrace their steps. There didn't seem to be a need for words. Time was nonexistent; so was the outside world. They were aware only of each other.

When they neared the entryway to Ariel's house,

Lacy's heart began to pound as a little spark of emotional reality reasserted itself. Would he want to come in? Would she let him? That would be such a commitment, and she wasn't sure she was ready yet.

Sloan halted beneath the covered portico, struggling with himself to keep cool. As a younger man he might have been unsuccessful. But if attaining the ripe age of thirty-one had taught him one thing, it was that patience always had its own reward. He limited himself to taking one of her hands in both of his. Anything more, and his straining need might burst the barrier he was valiantly trying to keep intact.

"Come out with me tomorrow," he urged huskily.

Lacy could see his face now; it was partially illuminated by the light coming from the living room window. She became lost in the carved handsomeness of his features and the very blueness of his eyes.

"Where?"

He shrugged slightly. "Anywhere."

"When?"

"Daybreak?"

"Don't—don't you have to work?"

An intrusive vision of Caroline pushed its way into his brain, but Sloan quickly forced it away. He didn't want to think of her now. He had only one purpose.

"No. It's my day off."

Lacy hesitated for a moment, the blood in her veins leaping instead of flowing smoothly.

"All right."

Sloan smiled, and it was enough to make her knees buckle. Whenever he smiled like that...

His warm fingers tightened on her own, and she prepared herself for another kiss. She wanted it. But he only continued to look down at her as a flash of some mysterious form of lightning escaped from the banked storm that was in his eyes.

Chapter Seven

If Lacy had never before experienced a waking dream, she certainly couldn't make claim to that feat any longer. Nothing about yesterday evening seemed real. It was as if it had all happened to someone else. Had Sloan really come? Had they talked, walked, kissed? Had she agreed to go out with him today at dawn's first light? How could such a turnaround have happened so quickly? Yesterday morning she had been content to keep him out of her life, had actively worked at doing so. Then, as soon as she saw him again, her defenses crumbled and she willingly allowed herself to be plunged into this topsy-turvy wonderland of confused feelings that were just as strong now as they had been then.

Lacy moved restlessly in the bed, kicking at the top sheet that insisted on wrapping itself about her ankles. Finally she gave up and pushed to a sitting position in the darkened room, swinging her feet to the carpet, being careful not to disturb the sleeping dog. She padded to the window and looked outside.

Everything was still covered in night; the moon had journeyed on. She had no idea what time it was. She glanced back toward the bedside clock. Four—it was four. It seemed as though it should be ten! But then if it were, she would be with Sloan, and only heaven knew what they would be doing.

Lacy's grasp tightened on the material of the curtain as an involuntary spark of remembered pleasure sped through her. She had earlier referred to what had passed between them as a kiss. That was like summing up the paintings on the ceiling of the Sistine Chapel as a nice collection of sketches. It had been much more than a simple kiss. If he had pressed the issue, she would have gladly had sex with him right then, right there, unmindful of the dog, of their being in the open, of the fact that she had been telling herself for the past two weeks that she didn't even like him. She would have done it and experienced no regrets. At least not until later, when the enormity of what she had done had seeped into her conscience. Thank heaven he had pulled away!

But why had he? She knew he had wanted her. There had been no mistaking that fact. He couldn't have hidden it if he tried. Lacy frowned. She might not be experienced in the physical act of lovemaking, but she knew enough about it—even if she had once thought herself above it—to know that they had been teetering on the brink, skating on the edge, playing with the flickering tongues of a fire that in all likelihood would consume them. Then he had stopped. Why?

She moved back to the edge of the bed and sank down on the soft coverlet. Sloan was an enigma to her. He said things, did things, that totally put her off balance. After getting into bed last night she had tried to tell herself that she still didn't like him, but she knew that wasn't completely true. And it wasn't because of the physical magnetism that seemed to assert itself each time they met. There had been that day in his office when all hell was breaking loose. He had smiled at her so whimsically, and silently welcomed her glimpse into a portion of his life. Then last night, sitting on the floor, drying the poodle...She had resented his interference, but she couldn't honestly say that she was sorry he was there.

He had asked her if she wanted a shining knight. Did she? Had that been what Richard was to her? Courtly, courteous, safe?

Lacy shook her head, making the long strands of her chestnut hair swing against her shoulders. No. She couldn't accept that. She had loved Richard. She still did. Only—only what kind of love had it been?

Restlessly she once again stood up. She wasn't going to think about that right now. She didn't want to think about anything too deeply. She was going to go into the bathroom, draw a hot tub, and then soak in it until an hour had gone by. And she wasn't going to allow any further misgivings to enter her thought processes. For once in her life she was going to float with the tide. She wasn't going to agonize over the pros and cons. She would keep her date with Sloan and to hell with logic, with propriety, and with what she could only describe as her previous snobbery.

The doorbell ran a short time after daybreak, causing Lacy's nerves to start their usual dance of anticipation at the near prospect of Sloan's presence. The fandango increased in its frenzy when she opened the door and saw him.

The first rays of morning sun caressed Sloan's features, making Lacy aware that he was even more handsome than she remembered. The stong, clean jaw was freshly shaven, a bright look was lighting the blue eyes, his hair was newly combed, with only a few of the gilded strands falling out of place in the soft westerly breeze, and the blue denim shirt with its sleeves rolled part way up his arms and the snugly-fitting faded jeans merely added to the picture of a man who enjoyed the out-of-doors. Lacy couldn't move her gaze for several appreciative seconds, then she gave a short, tentative smile and motioned him inside. The entryway seemed to be filled with his presence when he complied.

"Good morning," he greeted, his smile flashing white against his bronzed skin.

"Good morning," she returned, somewhat ill at ease because of her thoughts.

"Are you ready?"

Lacy looked down at her rust-colored jeans and white oxford shirt. "I wasn't sure how to dress."

She felt Sloan's eyes travel over her and her breath halted momentarily.

"You're perfect," he pronounced at last. Was there a hint of strained huskiness in his voice?

"Would you like a cup of coffee?" She offered the drink more to have something to say rather than as a means to delay their departure.

"No, not unless you do."

They were both being so fromal. "I just had one."

Sloan nodded, his eyes still on her face. Lacy moved uncomfortably from one foot to the other. She gave another short smile. "You never told me where we're going." There, that sounded fairly intelligent. And it would be nice to know.

Sloan tucked his fingers into the front pockets of his jeans. "Have you ever heard of Enchanted Rock?"

"Of course. I grew up here. It's close to Fredericksburg, isn't it?"

Again he nodded and seemed to put that little bit of information about her past down in his memory. Then he asked, "Have you ever climbed it?"

"Climbed it?"

"Yes."

"No."

"Do you have any objection to doing it today?"

Lacy didn't know that people could climb it. "No."

"Then that's what I thought we'd do. I was there before it was turned into a state park, when it was privately owned, but I haven't been back in ages. And you don't really have to worry about it being much of a climb. It's more like a hike up a steep incline." He paused. "You really should change your shoes though. Those won't work very well."

Lacy glanced down at her thin-strapped sandals. "Would tennis shoes do?"

"Sure, that's what I have on."

Lacy's gaze went to his feet and confirmed his words. "I'll go get mine." She started to turn away and then turned back. "You can wait in the living room if you like."

Some of the warmth of his smile came out to enfold her. "I'll be fine here."

Lacy's heart gave a somersault. Sloan should have to register that smile as a lethal weapon! She swung about and had started down the hall to her bedroom, when a

freshly awakened Sampson came hurrying from the
room to investigate the voices he had heard. He gave
her a sharp glance, then proceeded to the entryway
where he uttered one obligatory bark before starting a
jumping, tail-wagging, greeting to the vet. When she
turned out of the hall, Sloan was down on his haunches
trying to pet the enthusiastic blur.

It was only as Lacy was tying the final knot in her left
shoelace that the thought of what they were going to do
with Sampson occurred to her. From her memory of
where Fredericksburg was on the Texas map, it was at
least a good hundred miles away. They couldn't leave
the dog locked in the house all day, which was the
length of time they would need to drive over and back,
with climbing a mountain thrown in for good measure.
She didn't think it would be a good idea to take him.

Lacy hurried back to where she had left Sloan and
Sampson. The poodle had calmed a degree and was
now limiting himself to licking Sloan's face. Sloan
straightened at her approach.

"I've just thought of something—what am I going to
do with Sampson?"

"Not to worry, everything's under control. Just
leave it to Uncle Sloan. He can stay at the office. We'll
drop him off as we leave."

"You mean, board him there for the day?"

"You got it."

"But—"

"He'll be fine. And he'd be a lot better off there than
he would trying to keep up with us."

"But won't that be a lot of trouble? I mean—"

"I've already talked it over with Max. He's expecting
him."

Lacy could think of no other protest. The problem was solved. "Do I need to bring anything else?"

"Nope. It's all taken care of."

She tilted her head a degree. "You've planned for everything."

"I was a boy scout."

At that Lacy smiled. She could just see him in his uniform. "And once a boy scout, always a boy scout. Right?"

"Be prepared, that's my motto."

The car Sloan drove wasn't exactly a car. It was a Jeep—a Renegade—black, with bright orange and yellow stripes marking its sides.

"I could have brought my motorcycle," he explained. "But I didn't think you'd appreciate the long drive perched on the back."

"You thought right," Lacy agreed.

"You don't like motorcycles?"

"I think they're dangerous."

Sloan shrugged. "They're not so bad."

Lacy slid into the seat, holding Sampson on her lap, while Sloan slammed her door and came around to the driver's side.

"I don't suppose you like hang gliding either, then." He continued their conversation as he settled behind the wheel.

Now it was Lacy's turn to shrug. "I've never tried it. But I put it in the same category as jumping out of a perfectly sound airplane. Why would anyone do it?"

He started the engine. "Because of the thrill, the challenge. I've never sky dived, but hang gliding is so much like flying. For centuries man has tried to emulate the birds. Now he can. When you catch a good current, there's nothing but you and the sky. You see what the birds see, feel the—" He stopped and grinned. "Am I boring you?"

Lacy pretended to adjust Sampson's position on her lap. Him? Bore her? "No."

He put the car into gear and pressed the accelerator. "I get a little carried away sometimes."

She looked across at him as an idea sprang to her attention. "You're not going to hang glide today, are you? Off the mountain?"

Sloan laughed at that and spared a glance away from his driving. "No. I'd probably be arrested."

"Good."

Sloan directed the car around a corner. "Is that good that I'd be put in jail, or good that I'm not going to hang glide?"

"Exactly how high is this rock?"

"Several hundred feet."

"Are there places where you can fall off?"

"I suppose you could if you tried hard enough. Why?"

"Then I'm not going to answer your question. I want to get back to Austin in one piece."

"That could be a wise decision," he teasingly agreed.

When they drew into the veterinary office parking area, Sloan pulled the Renegade to a stop near the door.

"I'll just be a second. Come on, Sampson." The poodle willingly jumped into his grasp and Sloan walked away.

Lacy waited in silence, the early morning sun forcing her to turn toward the building. She watched as Sloan opened the door with his keys and disappeared within.

A few minutes later he was back, relocking the door, minus the dog. He walked to the Jeep with a healthy spring to his step.

After he resettled into position and started the engine, he flashed her another smile and began to whistle.

The drive to Fredericksburg was through country that was forever etched in Lacy's memory. No matter how long a person who was born and raised in the Central Texas hill country was away, he never forgot the rugged beauty of his dry, rocky homeland. The vista never changed. It had looked the same since the first time an Indian ventured into it. Then had come the Spanish and French explorers. Next the Mexicans and the Anglos. Each had carved only temporary memorials. In this land, man was merely a visitor.

They passed numerous signs that extolled the nearby L.B.J. Ranch that was now a national historic site. Then, as they approached a narrow Ranch Road that angled to the left, Sloan questioned, "Do you want to stop by Luckenbach? Like in the song Willie Nelson and Waylon Jennings sing?"

"Is there much to see?"

"Just a couple of old broken-down buildings."

"Are you saying that it's not much of a tourist mecca?"

"It had its day—"

"But the glory has passed."

Sloan grinned again, his eyes crinkling in the bright glare of the sun. "The only glory that place ever saw was in the song. Even in its heyday it never was much more than a dip in the road."

"I think I'll pass," she decided.

"Another wise choice."

Lacy looked at him curiously. "Then why did you ask?"

The Jeep passed the Ranch Road. "I'm just trying to oblige. Put it down to being a frustrated tour guide."

"But you don't have to do that with me. I'm a native, remember?"

"But you haven't climbed Enchanted Rock, you don't know what Luckenbach is like—"

"Neither do a lot of other native Texans." Lacy interceded. "And anyway, I haven't been away that long."

"Just how long is long?"

"Four years."

"What do you do in Boston? Or was it even Boston?"

"It was."

"So what do you do?"

A little tension suddenly sprang up between them. "I was a research assistant at a university."

"In what field?"

"Biochemistry."

"You have your degree?"

"A master's."

Sloan gave a low whistle. "Just how old *are* you?"

Lacy's chin lifted. She was accustomed to that question. "I'm twenty-six."

Sloan whistled again. "You've been a busy little girl."

"I am not a little girl!"

"Sorry."

A few silent miles went by. Then Lacy decided to

repay him in kind. "So what about you?" she challenged.

Sloan lifted a mock-puzzled eyebrow. She tightened her lips, but elucidated further, "How old are you?"

"I'm an old man. I'm thirty-one."

"Thirty-one isn't old."

"Sometimes it is."

"Are you from Austin?"

"Not originally. I was born in Temple, but my folks moved to Austin when I was five."

"So you were there when I was born."

"It looks that way."

Lacy was quiet a moment then spoke her thoughts out loud. "Isn't that strange? We both grew up in the same town and never met each other!"

"Austin is more a city than a town."

"Did you go to the University of Texas?"

He shook his head. "A & M."

"You're an Aggie!"

"Did you go to Texas?"

"Of course."

Sloan smiled widely. "Then it's no wonder we didn't get on at first. Subconsciously we must have known that we went to rival colleges."

"Yes. I've been told that Aggies have a certain— smell."

"Watch it. Remember the mountain."

Lacy pretended to be a repentant southern belle. "Oh, suh, ah am so sorry. Ah don't know what came over me. Why ah declare, sometimes my mouth just says things my mind didn't know it even knew."

Sloan's mouth pulled to one side. "That's the trouble with the people at Texas—they always like to talk when they don't have the slightest idea what they're talking about.''

Lacy immediately lost the thick accent. "You'd better watch it too," she warned. "Falling off Enchanted Rock can work two ways!"

They both broke into laughter, evaporating the remaining tension that had risen so quickly in the moments before.

The highway leading north out of Fredericksburg cut through a series of working ranches. But the land area of each was so large that very few signs of civilization besides an occasional intersecting fence and cattle guard gave evidence that people were about. The area seemed given over to an occasional cow and a multitude of buzzards who were enjoying the sport that Sloan seemed to love so much: hanging in the sky, moving from one heated updraft to another.

When Enchanted Rock first came into view, Lacy was startled by how impressive it looked. It was a monstrous dome of granite protruding out of the limestone around it like a bald, pink head. No vegetation seemed to break its stark lines. But as they covered more miles and came closer, Lacy could see the sporadic growth of brush—sometimes even an occasional stunted tree— that clung stubbornly to life in the fissures, especially along the rock's sloping base.

Sloan turned into the entrance and paid the small park fee, then he drew the Jeep to a halt in a parking area. As he withdrew the keys from the ignition he turned to her.

"Well, are you ready for this?"

"As ready as I'll ever be," she returned.

His approving smile washed over her. "Good. Then let's go."

He reached behind them into the rear seat and withdrew a backpack that Lacy had not previously noticed.

"Provisions," he explained.

She eyed the well-worn satchel. "Don't tell me—you like to tramp across country as well."

"Do you want me to lie?"

"No, just don't say anything."

Sloan gave a heartrending smile. "Mum's the word, then."

Lacy let herself out of the car and came around the rear to the driver's side where Sloan was just finishing pulling the pack onto his back. While he adjusted the shoulder straps he looked at her narrowly. Then he said,

"I forgot to ask. You did eat breakfast, didn't you?"

"A little."

"What did you have?"

Lacy felt a tinge of irritation, but tried to mask it. "A piece of toast."

"A piece of toast," he repeated disbelievingly. "A piece of toast. You're going to climb a mountain on a piece of toast!"

Her irritation increased. "Well, I didn't know I was going to climb one when I ate it. And, anyway, I'm not used to having breakfast so early."

"Could you eat something now?"

"Possibly."

"Then, here." He shrugged out of the pack and, opening the flap, dug through the contents until he came out with a small plastic Baggie. "Eat this. It'll give you energy."

Lacy took the proffered bag and examined it while Sloan redonned the pack.

"What is it?"

"Gorp."

"Gorp?"

"Good old raisins and peanuts, with some M&M's thrown in. Eat it."

Lacy undid the plastic top and took a tentative taste. The flavor combination was delicious. "Hey, it's good!" she exclaimed.

"Did you think I'd give you something that would taste bad?"

"Well—"

"Are you always this picky with your food?"

"It's my one big failing," Lacy laughed. "I don't like my spaghetti and my sauce to touch, either."

"God!"

"I know. That used to drive my sister wild."

Sloan took her arm, and they began to walk along the trail that led across a narrow stream and wound its way to where the ascent began. "I hope you like chicken sandwiches."

"Why?"

"Because that's what I made for us to eat up there." He motioned toward the unseen summit.

"And if I don't?"

"Then you'll have to make do with another one of those."

Lacy looked down at what remained of the "gorp". "I could do that. But as it happens, chicken sandwiches are my favorite."

Sloan made a satisfied sound and squeezed her arm.

The climb itself started out easier than Lacy thought it would. Everything was at an angle, and it required a constant uphill effort, but it wasn't that bad. All they had to do was follow the occasional faded painted arrow that marked an invisible path in the granite. Then the arrows became even more sparse, and they were left to make their way as best they could.

When at last they approached a flattened area, Lacy was winded and dropped to take a rest on a convenient upthrust rock that marked a fissure. Sloan lowered the pack and stretched out on the sun-warmed surface at her feet, his long legs before him, his shoulder propped against her rock.

Lacy looked down at him, mentally comparing their outward appearances. She knew she looked exhausted. Her cheeks were exuding enough warmth so that she didn't have to feel them to know they were flushed, and her breath was coming in quick, tight gasps. But Sloan—Sloan was hardly bothered. He looked as if he could have run from the base to where they were now and not even known that he had done it.

"Would you like something to drink?" he asked.

"Is it much further to the top?"

"Further than it looks, but not too far. Just a couple more rises."

Lacy thought for a moment then shook her head. "No, I can wait." She transferred her gaze to the view stretching out before them. From their heightened position, mile upon mile could be seen of the surrounding vista. It was almost overpoweringly lonely. And so very silent. They could have been transported back to another day in history, anywhere from Stone Age man to the more recent Comanche possession. Nothing had changed. The same rocks were present, the same grasses; the same warm breeze that blew in ages past was now disturbing her hair and Sloan's—Lacy had never before felt so close to nature. In Boston she had felt close to history, but it wasn't quite the same thing. This was old—older than time.

Sloan's thoughts must have been running parallel to her own, because he mused softly, "It's hard to deny the existence of a Creator when you're up here, isn't it?"

His words were almost worshipful. Lacy's held the same awe. "I feel like I can touch the sky."

Again they were silent, the smell of heated granite and dust mingling to add to the moment. Then Sloan moved, shifting position until he could look up at her as well.

"The Indians wouldn't come here at night. They wouldn't come anywhere near."

"Oh?"

Sloan nodded. "That's how the place got its name. They used to think the sounds the rock gave as it cooled from the heat of day were spirits. It's an eerie kind of moaning. I know because I've camped out here before."

The flesh along Lacy's arms prickled. "I think I'd agree with the Indians."

"Are you superstitious?"

Lacy's chin lifted. "A little."

"So am I, but not about that. I won't wear anything except a certain shirt when I hang glide. It's the one I learned in. When it wears out, I'll carry a little piece of it in my pocket. It's my luck."

Lacy relaxed a degree. So he wasn't going to harass her for being superstitious and instead was admitting to the partial insanity himself.

"I don't like black cats," she confided.

He smiled. "Is that all?"

Lacy rubbed at an imaginary speck of dirt on the leg of her jeans. "No, there's more. I know it's stupid, but I can't seem to help it. Dark, enclosed places like caves bother me."

She looked up to see him smile. "Caves?" he questioned. "How is that a superstition?"

"Aren't superstitions unnatural fears of ordinary things because something bad *might* happen?"

"Yes. I guess that would be a definition."

"Then caves are one of mine. When I was small my family and I went exploring in one once, by ourselves. It was on the property of a friend of my father's. I haven't liked them ever since."

"Wouldn't that be more of a phobia?"

Lacy couldn't help the shudder she gave as she remembered. "I really don't care what it is. All I know is that I don't like them."

"Don't you think you're being a little unrealistic? You said you were very young."

"Will you give me your shirt?"

"No."

"Then?"

He gave a slow smile. "Then I say we've reached an impasse."

Lacy smiled as well, and suddenly all thought of her fear of caves left her as the heat from the sun shining down upon them caused her uneasiness to melt away. Sloan was smiling up at her, his eyes creased from the

glare, the rays of bright light turning his hair to yellow
tongues of flame—and Lacy wanted to reach out to
him. She wanted to touch him. She liked the way his
long, lean body looked as it was resting with unconscious appeal so very close to her, liked the way his tan
was a vibrant golden brown, liked the way his hands
were sensitive yet strong. What would it hurt if she ran
a fingertip along his jaw? What would it hurt if she
leaned forward, just a little, and touched her mouth to
his?

Her breathing quickened at the mere thought, and to
cover the dangerous path her mind was following, she
stood up and tramped around a bit as if trying to work
the kinks out of abused muscles. The granite was reas-
suringly hard beneath her feet.

Sloan watched her actions from his position against
the raised rock. What had brought that on? One moment she seemed completely content, relaxing from
her surprising admission of fear, and the next she was
off and moving as if startled by something. Did it have
anything to do with the quicksilver flash of intense feeling he had seen for a few seconds in her eyes? And did
it concern him? Was it an awareness of him?

He moved effortlessly to his feet, a glimmer of expectancy lightening his soul. He wouldn't press the
issue now. He would go on as he had been. She was
opening up to him a degree. And even though he
wanted more—much more—he couldn't extinguish
completely the surge of happiness his speculation about
her action brought. Maybe it wasn't fair to her, but he
felt something like a marauding tiger who had just de-
tected a sign of vulnerability in his prey. The hunger
was still there, but with continued patience Sloan knew
he would soon see an end to it.

"Are you ready to move on?" he questioned easily, his hands coming to rest with unintentional grace on his slim hips.

Lacy glanced back at him, then transferred her attention to the unseen summit. "Sure. Are you?"

"As ready as I'll ever be."

She felt him move toward her and started walking herself. She didn't want him too close right then. She needed more time to regroup her faltering emotions.

As Sloan had said, the distance to the top was deceiving. Every time it looked as if the summit would surely be seen over the next high area, they discovered that there was yet another rise.

Finally they arrived at their destination, and Lacy dropped to the hard surface, once again feeling the effects of too many hours behind a desk and a microscope. Lord, she wasn't that old! Twenty-six wasn't exactly over the hill, but she was wheezing as if she were eighty. And Sloan? She let her eyes lift to his chest to make the comparison. Sloan was barely breathing hard. He was accustomed to activity, to sport. Yet he dropped down beside her, more, she knew, to be companionable than out of necessity.

"Well, what do you think?" he asked.

Lacy couldn't conceal her tiredness. She didn't really care about the view any longer. "I think I'd like that drink you offered earlier."

Sloan laughed and shifted the back pack from its resting place. "You're a little out of condition," he observed as he withdrew a thermos.

She took the cup from him as soon as he had finished pouring the water and raised it thirstily to her lips. She let the comment pass while she drank her fill.

When she was finished she handed the cup back and wiped her mouth with her fingers. Then she was ready to reply.

"When you spend most of your available time in a laboratory, you do tend to get a little out of shape."

Sloan resisted the impulse to say that it wasn't her shape he had been referring to, that her curves had absolutely nothing wrong with them.

Instead he inquired, "What kind of research do you do?"

"Did—I *did* research."

"What happened?"

Lacy shrugged. "It ended."

"Did you enjoy your work?"

"Yes."

"Have you tried to find another position?"

"No."

"Why?"

Lacy tried to change the subject. "Don't you want something to drink yourself?"

"I'll have some in a minute. Answer my question."

"I'm not afraid of heights."

Sloan studied her tightened face carefully, then he laughed, trying to ease her tension. "What does that have to do with anything?"

"It means I don't need any help in getting down. I can go right this minute if I want."

"Is that your way of telling me to mind my own business?"

"You could say that."

"Well, you started it. I didn't bring up your work. You did. I was just curious."

Lacy gave an exasperated sigh. He was doing it

again—twisting and turning until she didn't know up from down. But he did have a point. Maybe she was being too touchy.

"I haven't applied anywhere else because there hasn't been that much time."

"Your job ended suddenly?"

"The professor I worked with died."

In the silence that followed Lacy wished the words unsaid. How could she talk about Richard so—so easily? And with Sloan. She clasped her hands together over her updrawn knees and looked unseeingly out over the surrounding landscape. A rinse of tears rose to her eyes, but she blinked them away. She hadn't cried for weeks; she wasn't about to now.

Sloan sensed her pain. There was something here. Something she didn't want to confide. Something about the man she had worked with. A burning jealousy began to grow in his chest. Had she loved this other man? Had they had a close relationship? An intimate relationship? He had to fight to keep from demanding an answer.

With a shortness that was uncommon to him, he questioned, "Have you seen enough?"

Lacy nodded.

"Then let's get the hell off this rock."

At the unaccustomed anger he was displaying, Lacy glanced quickly around.

Sloan met her questioning gaze and his conscience began to reproach him. It wasn't her fault that he was behaving irrationally—like a spoiled brat who had discovered that his prize was less than perfect. By what right did he expect her to be perfect? He wasn't. And he was proving it with each succeeding second. Why did he sometimes seem to go out of his way to alienate her? If he let himself think too deeply he might come up with an answer, so he quickly mollified himself with the excuse that he wasn't always the easiest person to live with. His eyes softened and he apologized, "I'm sorry."

"For what?"

"For acting like a bear with a sore behind."

Lacy blinked, then gave a tentative giggle that soon turned into the real thing. "I've never heard that one before."

"It's an old vet joke."

"From A&M?"

"No, from a friend of mine." When his conscience pricked again, Sloan winced inwardly, but he refused to let his thoughts of Jim, not to mention any whisper of Caroline, gain a foothold in his mind. He smiled and teased, "Aggie jokes are better."

"Like how?" She smiled encouragement.

"Have you ever heard the one about the Aggies who were riding in a pickup truck that drove into a lake?"

"No."

His smile deepened in anticipation. "The two in the cab got out okay, but the ones in back drowned because they couldn't get the tailgate open."

Lacy thought for a moment, then burst into appreciative laughter. "They couldn't get the—oh, my lord, Sloan. That's bad!"

"What is a mosquito called that flies into an Aggie's ear?" He waited a second. "A space invader."

Lacy nearly collapsed. In fact she did, rolling over onto her side.

"Do you want to hear another?"

Lacy shook her head. "No. Stop. I—"

"A pot of gold is in the center of a room. Santa Claus is in one corner, the Easter Bunny is in another, a smart Aggie is in yet another and a dumb Aggie is in the last. Which one will get the pot of gold?" He paused, but it wasn't long enough for Lacy to make a guess, even if she could. "The dumb Aggie, of course," he answered. "The other three are mythical characters."

Lacy struggled to sit up. "Please," she begged, "you have to stop!"

Sloan was enjoying her misery. Telling Aggie jokes was like eating potato chips: It was impossible to tell just one. But finally he conceded.

Lacy was wiping at her eyes, trying to clear her vision, when Sloan made the disclaimer, "They're pretty old. Made the rounds a long time ago."

She sniffed. "They're new to me."

"You've been away."

She took a deep breath. She didn't remember when she had last laughed so hard. "Since when have Aggies been the ones to tell Aggie jokes? I thought all of you hated them."

Sloan started to rummage in the backpack again. "If a person or group can't laugh at themselves, they might as well give up. They're taking things too seriously. I've always enjoyed Aggie jokes, even when I was at school. In fact, I've been responsible for coming up with a few new ones myself."

"One of those?"

"No, mine weren't exactly the kind I'd want to repeat right now."

"They were a little too rough around the edges?"

"Crude would be more accurate."

"You've gotten my interest. Come on. Tell me one. Edit if you feel you have to."

Sloan chuckled. "No, I don't want to embarrass myself."

"You don't think you might embarrass me?"

"If I would, you wouldn't have asked."

So much for that. Lacy wasn't going to press further. And, unwillingly, she had to admit that she liked his logic.

When Sloan was through withdrawing articles from the pouch, a meal was set before them. Chicken sandwiches, as he had earlier promised, two apples, and a Hershey's bar each came from an insulated cold pack, as well as the remaining bag of "gorp." Cans of Coke that had been frozen, then allowed to thaw in the day's heat, rounded off the repast.

At first sight of the amount of food, Lacy had almost made the mistake of saying that she couldn't possibly eat so much. But after the first taste of her sandwich, she was glad that she hadn't said anything. The crisp, fresh air and the work involved in climbing to the summit had brought out her appetite, and she kept pace with Sloan bite for bite.

Chapter Eight

Later, as the miles leading back into Austin were being retraced, Lacy was grateful that she had made the decision to enjoy such a large lunch, because it seemed that the granite mountain wasn't the only difficult-to-get-to site Sloan was going to encourage her to see that day. And what made the situation even worse was that from the way he described Balanced Rock, she was just as enthusiastic as he to climb another incline to appreciate it.

Their destination was on the same Ranch Road that led to the mountain of granite, only closer to the town of Fredericksburg, and the going was much rougher. More brush to pass through, more jagged pieces of steep granite to scale. This was no gentle incline that allowed an easy walk.

Possibly it was due to the fact that by this time antiquity in nature was beginning to wear a little thin—possibly because it seemed to Lacy as if every muscle in her body was aching, especially those in her legs—but the huge red boulder, sitting poised on an unbelievably narrow point where it had stood for thousands of years, was a disappointment. All she could think of was a tub

filled to the brim with hot bubbly water, and herself
with the time to spend the rest of her life leisurely relaxing in it.

Sloan must have sensed her growing exhaustion, because they didn't tarry as long in further examination
of the second area as they had at the first. And on the
journey home, he remained quiet, letting her rest.

With her head propped on the rear cushion of the
seat, Lacy closed her eyes. She was content for the
miles to pass while she reflected on the day she had
spent. Her muscles were tired—she would probably
hobble for a week—but she had enjoyed it. She would
never be an outdoor person, preferring instead four
walls and a challenging experiment, but being with
Sloan, enjoying what he enjoyed, had made the day
special. Grudgingly she admitted that she was beginning to like what she was coming to know about him.

It was one thing to be unwillingly attracted to a person on a physical level and another to find that you
liked the person as a person. That led the relationship
to a new, higher dimension.

Somehow, coming to that conclusion as the Jeep's
engine hummed and the exercise of the day lulled her
mind and body into a floaty kind of prelude to sleep,
Lacy was not as frightened as she might have been
another time.

On hearing her soft sigh Sloan swiveled his gaze
from the road ahead, just as it had been wont to do with
increasing frequency as the slender, feminine body
seated next to him slipped deeper into a restful silence.
When he saw the even tenor of her breathing and knew
that she was asleep, his hands tightened on the wheel.

OK, old son, he berated himself in disgust, now that

you've half killed her, do you think she'll ever want to go out with you again? His look went over the chestnut head that turned away from him. Ha! Fat chance! he answered his own question. She'd probably be afraid you'd enter her in a marathon.

Sloan cursed himself. He had known that she was unaccustomed to hiking and climbing. She had told him so. But he didn't let the day stop with climbing one mountain. Oh, no, he had to make her climb two. If she even spoke to him again it would be a miracle.

The change in the Jeep's speed and motion as it turned into the subdivision disturbed Lacy's consciousness enough to awaken her. For a moment she was unsure of where she was, then realization came back with a thump at the same second as the front tire managed to find a pothole.

"Oh!" Lacy exclaimed, struggling to sit upright. She glanced over at Sloan who was scowling.

"Sorry," he muttered almost under his breath.

Lacy straightened her limp blouse, still feeling a bit woozy. She was embarrassed that she had fallen asleep.

"I'm the one who should be sorry," she apologized. "I didn't mean to fall asleep. I don't normally do that."

If she had thought to cheer him with that interesting piece of news, her hopes were immediately dashed. His scowl deepened even more, causing her to lapse into another silence, angry with herself for spoiling what had been a very nice day. From his point of view the drive back couldn't have been very stimulating. Not many men would feel complimented by having their companion of the day fall as soundly asleep as a rock. Oh, no! Lacy brought herself up. Not a rock. Anything but a rock! Her mouth pulled into a reflexive smile, and she couldn't control the small sound that escaped her throat.

Sloan instantly turned to look at her, his blue eyes widening with some amazement. She was laughing?

Lacy peered across at him. She didn't want him to think that she was laughing at him. So when she saw his interested look, she fabricated a little.

"I was just thinking about what a nice day this has been."

After a moment some of the tension that had been about Sloan's mouth was released. "And you laughed?"

"I've had fun," she explained. "I don't think I want to climb anything higher than a curb for a while, but, all in all, this has been quite an experience. Thank you."

The black cloud that Sloan had been existing under for almost a hundred miles evaporated into nothingness. A smile began to crinkle the corners of his eyes and caused the creases in his cheeks to deepen. "I'm relieved to hear you say that. I was afraid you'd hated it."

"No," Lacy quickly denied.

"Then you'll come out with me again?"

"To do what?"

Sloan appreciated her caution. "How about a nice dinner? Those sandwiches on the mountain were filling but that was about all."

"You mean tonight?"

"Sure, why not?" Strike while the iron was hot, wasn't that the old saying?

Lacy hesitated. "Well—"

"I promise you won't have to do anything more strenuous than lift your fork."

How could she refuse? "All right. But I need about an hour to clean up."

Sloan turned his attention from the road long enough to examine his own slightly rumpled self. "Me too."

"Then it's a date," Lacy agreed and felt a ridiculous elation. She especially felt it when those magnetic blue eyes gave her a short yet penetrating glance before going back to the road.

Sampson was on his dignity upon returning to his home. He hadn't liked being caged all day, and he wasn't about to let Lacy forget it. All the while she soaked in the tub trying to loosen sore muscles and grime, he lay on the bathroom floor, his silver body flat, his chin resting on the tile, his long fluffy ears spread out on either side of his face, with a reproachful look in his eyes.

"Sampson, I've already told you I'm sorry," Lacy said from the tub. "But you wouldn't have liked doing what we did today. I promise you. Your little feet would have fallen off. You were much better off where you were. Believe me."

The poodle didn't so much as blink. He just kept looking at her. Lacy gave a great sigh. Aristocratic poodledom had been offended and wasn't going to give in easily.

"I'll take you for a long walk tomorrow," she bribed, her attention moving to the especially large bubble that was floating beside her toe. With one quick jab she popped it. Sampson made no move.

Lacy looked back at him. "All right. Have it your own way. But I refuse to feel guilty because I left you." She paused. "And you're probably not going to like being left again tonight. But I'm going to do it. You'll just have to adjust yourself.''

With that Lacy hardheartedly continued her bath, ignoring the dog's pout. Sloan would be here at seven thirty. She couldn't take any more time in trying to mollify her canine friend.

By some miracle Lacy was ready at seven thirty. There had been a great debate about what she would wear, but she finally settled on a summery dress in a clear shade of yellow that complemented her skin as well as her eyes. Yet maybe it was excitement that was lending her eyes that special sparkle. They were definitely brighter than usual. She had decided to wear her hair pulled into a high coronet on top of her head. It wasn't a style she was accustomed to wearing, but she knew it looked appealing.

Not that she wanted to look appealing, she reassured herself. That was the furthest thing from her mind. She just wanted to look nice, different from the way she had looked his morning and this afternoon.

When the doorbell rang, Lacy's heart gave a quick little jump and she had to swallow before she could move to answer it. What was she getting so worked up about? The last time she had seen Sloan had been only an hour before. Sampson roused from his sulk long enough to accompany her.

Sloan waited outside the door, experiencing a nervousness like none he had ever known before. Then, as the door opened, he instantly knew the cause. Lacy was beautiful, the most beautiful woman he had ever seen.

If telepathy had been in vogue Lacy would have

echoed his thoughts. He was magnificent! The last time she had seen him in a suit was in the airplane. And then she hadn't been too willing to concede his good points. But now—a weak tremor started in her knees and worked its way through her body into her fingers. She clutched the doorknob even tighter to conceal her trembling as she met the intensity of his eyes.

For a moment neither of them seemed able to move. It took Sampson to break the tension that had sprung up between them. He moved slowly over the threshold, rose up on his rear legs, and gave one sharp, imperious bark. If these humans could lock him away all day, the least they could do now was give him the attention he felt he deserved.

He received his wish. Both Lacy and Sloan looked down at him and Sampson could hold out no longer. He had punished them enough. A wag of his tail showed his forgiveness, and soon he was back to being his usual lovable self.

Sloan bent down to reach for him at the same instant as Lacy. Their hands met on the silver hair. A thousand electrified sparks might have jumped from one to the other. Reacting instinctively Lacy jerked her hand away and straightened. Sloan was slower to follow her lead, but he eventually stood up as well, lifting the poodle in his arms. He carried him into the house and shut the door behind them.

Lacy was standing before a narrow table, her back to the entryway. But she knew every move Sloan was making, could feel the burning touch of his eyes.

Sloan's gaze almost devoured her slender form. He wanted to forget about going out to eat tonight. There were many much more interesting possibilities that could be looked into. And he knew that she wasn't immune. But he held onto his tongue with difficulty and, instead, concentrated on showering affection on the dog.

Lacy turned around when she had herself under some kind of control again. Had today only been a prelude to tonight? "He wasn't very happy about being left," she imparted, more for something to say than for importance. "I think we injured his dignity."

Sloan lowered the little dog to the carpet. "We're going to injure it even more tonight." Was he hoping she would suggest not going out herself?

She tried to keep herself from staring at how good he looked in his dark suit. The color contrasted perfectly with his light hair. "Yes." She agreed, her heart beating loudly, while a wild humming started in her ears.

He waited for her to continue. When she didn't, he spoke into the lengthening silence. "I suppose we'd better go. Our reservation's for eight." He wasn't surprised by the low huskiness of his words.

Both of them were overwhelmingly aware that there was something so tangible going on between them that if either reached out to touch it they might discover it for what it was. But each made the struggle to resist, and finally they were able to leave it behind—at least for a time.

"I'll get my purse," Lacy decided, then pressed her lips together to keep them steady.

The restaurant Sloan took her to was a quietly understated building located close to the capitol. Its interior was equally restrained, yet exuding a friendly sort of intimacy. The decor was simple, which made it all the more impressive.

Seated in her chair, Lacy examined her surroundings. The predominant color was white: white linen table-cloths and napkins, white wicker chairs, white woven baskets strategically placed around the room to hold an immense variety of contrasting green plants and indoor trees. The only bright accent was the thick red candle resting in a beautiful brass holder and surrounded by a ring of freshly arranged white carnations which was placed on each table as a centerpiece.

"Do you like seafood?"

Sloan's question caused Lacy to start inwardly. Very little conversation had passed between them since leaving Ariel's home.

"Most kinds, yes."

"Have you ever tried stuffed flounder?"

"No."

Sloan lowered the menu. "It's fresh from the Gulf, and I can vouch for its being delicious."

Lacy didn't think she could eat anything. Coming here had been a terrible mistake. She should have begged off and curled up in bed with a book, even if it was one of Ariel's romances.

"That sounds fine to me."

Sloan smiled, and her stomach curled into even more knots. Ever since they had touched when reaching for Sampson she had been in a perpetual state of tension.

"Good." When the waiter came Sloan gave their order, all the while checking with her as to her further desires.

Lacy attached her gaze to the carnations once they

were alone again. Sloan's blue eyes roved over her,
over her hair, her face, and finally the smooth skin of
her shoulders the summery dress revealed. He felt an
immediate physical reaction that caused him to shift
uncomfortably in his seat.

"At least it's not crowded in here tonight," he said
to fill in space. "On weekends it's hard to get a table.
Between the college kids and the bureaucrats, it's kept
filled."

She nodded.

"It hasn't been open long, but word of mouth has
spread," he added.

Lacy fingered her glass.

He sighed to himself. She was drawing away from
him again. He would have to do something to shake
her out of it. He decided to go directly to the heart of
the problem. "You're very quiet. Do you want to
leave?"

Lacy glanced up startled, her eyes large. Had she
been that obvious? "No. No, I—"

"You're probably worn out," he interrupted her denial. "I'll cancel the order and take you home."

She studied his serious expression. Candlelight was
supposed to do wonderful things for a woman, but she
found that it did wonderful things for a man as well.
Somehow Sloan contrived to look more vital than ever.
The rich glow emphasized the golden hues of his tan,
the well-drawn sculpture of the planes of his face, the
sensuous and sensitive mouth, the straight nose, and,
as ever, the unusually vivid color of his eyes.

"No." She made the sudden decision. "I'm fine.
Really, I want to stay."

A slow smile spread on his lips and she couldn't help

but wonder if he had known exactly how she felt all along and only offered tiredness as an excuse. When he reached out to lift the drink from her hand, then followed the move with a reassuring squeeze, she wondered even more.

"Have I told you yet that you look very beautiful?"

The huskily spoken question sent a path of molten sensation through Lacy's body. She couldn't look away from his eyes.

"You do. I like your hair up like that." His smile became tender. "It kind of makes you look like an innocent sophisticate—a contradiction—a woman of the world, yet one who still hasn't been touched by any form of harsh reality."

Lacy's yellowish eyes darkened until there was a great deal of brown, her thoughts centering immediately on Richard.

Sloan noted her almost imperceptible wince and murmured softly, "Or have you?"

Lacy tugged at her hand, but his fingers would not release their hold. "Please," she whispered.

"Is it that professor? The one who died. Was he something special to you, Lacy?"

Lacy jerked her hand again, only this time with more determination, and Sloan let her escape. When she remained stubbornly silent, Sloan reattached the restraints of his mingled curiosity and jealousy and let his hand come back to his side of the table. Now wasn't the time to press further. It was too soon. If he continued, he would only drive her further away.

The arrival of their meal helped smooth over the strained feelings of the last few moments. Lacy still didn't feel like food, not even when she tasted the deliciously prepared flounder filled with crab meat. But she forced down a few bites, just to show that she was not shaken by his perceptiveness.

Sloan kept the conversation light throughout the rest of the meal. He seemed not to notice that she was hardly eating or that her replies were short and economical. His strategy worked. Soon, without her really being aware of what was happening, she was relaxing, and by the time their after-dinner coffee had arrived, she was even laughing at some of the outrageous tales he was sharing about the trials and tribulations of being a vet.

"I've never read any of the James Herriot books," she confided, a smile still lingering about her mouth as she named the famed English veterinarian who specialized in sharing his experiences in print. "But I did see an excerpt in a magazine—*Reader's Digest* or somewhere—and it sounds as if you two have a lot in common."

Sloan sat back in his seat. "All vets do. But, yes, I like Herriot. He has a special sensitivity and can see the humor in little things. He also has a way with words that most people don't."

Lacy tilted her head to one side and teased, "You've never been tempted to jot a few things down yourself?"

He gave a short laugh. "When I string five words together it's a miracle. I have a friend who's almost disowned me because its been so long since I've written."

"Oh?"

He nodded. "He's the best letter writer of all time. Once I finally do manage to come up with something to send, he answers so quickly I get discouraged. Then he writes and takes me to task for not writing." He shook his head in memory.

"Ariel thinks I don't write enough either, or telephone."

"My friend lives in Saudi Arabia. He's with an oil company there."

"No wonder you don't call. I was about to suggest that. Now I'm glad I didn't."

Sloan continued his part of the conversation, satisfied that he had her talking again. "Did Ariel take the news about Sampson well?" he asked easily, comfortably.

Lacy grimaced. "As well as can be expected. She's called almost every day, checking on how he's doing. I've tried to tell her he's fine, but she's just like a mother hen, worrying because she isn't here to see for herself."

"My offer still stands, I'll talk to her if you like."

"Oh, no. That's just Ariel's way. She believes me, she just thinks she has to call."

He nodded, then became serious. "When you see the number of animals that come into our offices because their owners don't care, you might not feel your sister is so overprotective. I wish there were more like her." He shook himself free of his depressing thoughts and gave a deprecating shrug. "Not a very good subject to end a meal on, I'm afraid."

Lacy watched him levelly. Then she heard herself ask, "What made you want to become a vet?"

Sloan took another sip of his coffee. When the cup was safely resting in its saucer once again, he answered, "I don't really know. I've worked with animals for as long as I can remember."

"Was your father a vet?"

He gave a harsh laugh. "My father was a bum." At her indrawn breath of surprise he enlightened her further. "He drank like there was no tomorrow and couldn't keep a job, until finally no one would hire him. My mother supported us by taking in other people's kids. Then one day he left. We never heard from him again."

Lacy was startled. She would never have suspected him of having such a background. He seemed so assured, so accustomed to the nicer things of life.

"That must have been hard."

Sloan grimaced. "It was harder when he was there. After he disappeared, Mom got a job at a supermarket, and I started working in a nearby veterinary office. We were a lot better off, both emotionally and financially."

"How—how old were you?"

"Eleven, twelve. I can't remember."

"Is your mother—?" She couldn't complete the question. It was none of her business really.

"She died three years ago. And she wasn't still checking groceries!"

No, Lacy thought, I bet she wasn't. Once Sloan had made his way in the world, his mother would never have had to worry about another thing. She knew that without being told.

"I'm glad."

"Why?"

She proceeded cautiously. "Because I believe it meant a lot to you."

Sloan relaxed tensed muscles that he hadn't known he had tensed. "You're right. It meant a hell of a lot."

A little silence descended, both of them dealing with

private thoughts, then Sloan pushed his coffee away and signaled for the bill.

The drive back to Ariel's was as silent as the previous trip into Austin. But this time Lacy wasn't dwelling on her physical reactions to the man seated next to her. This time she was thinking of him as a little boy, of how difficult his life must have been. He probably would never admit it—not to someone he barely knew—but she could imagine the hurt involved, the pain. Twelve years wasn't very old to have to face life as an adult. He hadn't mentioned brothers or sisters, so she assumed he was an only child. And that, as she was coming to know him, meant that he would have tried his very best to become the man of the family. Lacy thought about his mother and wondered what she had been like. To have raised a son as strong and caring as Sloan, she must have been a very special person, especially when she had to work to overcome his father's negative image.

For his part Sloan was involved in serious thoughts, too. If his mother were alive, what would she think about what he was doing? Would she understand? Would she see that he seemed compelled to be with Lacy? What advice would she give him?

Almost automatically Sloan directed the Jeep into the subdivision. Then he slowed their progress as an idea occurred. "Lacy?"

Lacy turned her head, rousing herself from her contemplations. She waited for him to speak.

"I have something I want to give you."

She blinked at the unexpected sentence.

"You do?"

Sloan gave a slow smile. She could see it reflected in

the light as they passed a street lamp. "Don't be so surprised. It's not all that much. Just a book."

"What kind of book?"

"One of James Herriot's."

Lacy straightened. "You don't have to do that."

"I know I don't. I want to."

A frown settled on Lacy's brow as the Jeep slowed even more and turned into the parking area of a group of apartments.

"Where are we going?"

"To get the book."

"And where is the book?"

"In my apartment."

A shiver of apprehension slid down Lacy's spine. "Your apartment," she repeated.

Sloan parked the Jeep then looked at her quizzically. "You didn't expect me to produce it out of thin air, did you?"

Lacy was suitably embarrassed. "No, but—"

A stillness came over Sloan. "Look. I'm not trying to take you someplace to ravish you. If I wanted to do that, I could do it anywhere. You'll be just as safe in my apartment as you are anywhere with me."

Feeling slightly ridiculous, Lacy was unsure of what to say.

"Come on. Trust me," he prompted. "I promise I won't pounce on you the instant the door closes."

But what if she were to pounce on him? Was that what was worrying her? Lacy applied a mental brake. She had to treat this situation as coolly as he did.

"I'm not worried about that," she assured him.

"OK, then, let's go."

He suited action to his words and exited from the

car. Lacy followed his lead, only somewhat more slowly. She still wasn't completely sure. Then she gave herself an emotional pep talk. How old was she? Twenty-six. How long had she made her way in the world practically alone, living in Boston, working for her own support? Four years, regardless of the fact that they had been a very protected four years—years spent with her eye to a test tube, so to speak. And did she want him to think she was afraid? Lord, no!

She straightened her shoulders and followed him past a set of stairs and under a raised walkway. He stopped at a door with the number 101 emblazoned on its surface and brought up his keys.

Lacy knew she had lived a very sterile life up to now, but this was the first time she had been in a man's apartment, and it was hard for her to act as if it weren't. But she did. She gave a calm look around, noting that Sloan was a very neat person. Nothing was piled or stacked. The soft leather couch in light camel, the matching chairs, the glass-topped occasional table that sat in front of each, the tasteful brass lamp that arced from a pedestal on the floor, the beautifully papered walls that looked like pressed cane—the entire effect was very pleasing to the eye.

"It's very nice," she complimented him, clinging to her calm.

"Thanks," he murmured as he watched her move further into the room. She stopped before a framed Monet print.

"Very nice," she said again.

Sloan bowed his head slightly in acknowledgement. He was aware of her nervousness. Someone less sensitive to another's deepest emotions might not have noticed, but his entire career was focused on being attuned. He knew. But he made no comment. She was like a newly gentled filly; one wrong move and all his hard work and patience would be wasted.

"Would you like something to drink? I have some liquor I keep for guests."

Lacy stilled the trembling of her limbs with difficulty. She was aware of him in every atom of her body. "No, I don't think so."

His gaze narrowed on her back. "Coffee?"

Lacy drew a deep breath and turned to face him, her hazel eyes large as she gave a small smile. "I don't want anything, thank you."

Sloan had to bite his tongue to keep from saying that that definitely wasn't his problem, not with her standing there looking so appealing. He knew exactly what he wanted! Instead he said, "I'll go get the book."

He was gone for only a few moments and when he returned, she was still positioned where he had left her. He moved close and handed her the hardcover copy of *All Things Bright and Beautiful.*

Lacy glanced from the book up into his eyes. She was unable to sustain his gaze and looked back down again, for the moment seeing nothing more than a blur. What was the matter with her? Why did she feel so close to crying? Was it because he was giving her something of his? Did it mean that much to her?

Lacy covered her temporary emotionalism by opening the cover, intent on flipping through a few pages before making some kind of safe comment. But as the book opened, her attention was drawn to a signature. For several seconds she studied it and then her eyes flew upward once again. Sloan was watching her steadily.

"It's signed!"

He smiled. "Yes."

"By Herriot."

Sloan's smile increased. "Yes again."

"I can't take it."

"Why not?"

"Because he autographed it for you!"

Sloan took the book from her hands. "No, look again. It's just signed. I have a friend in England who met him once and had him sign it. He sent it on to me because he thought I'd enjoy having it."

"And you don't?"

"Of course I do."

"Then why give it to me?"

"Because I want to."

Lacy took the book that was once again proffered. As had happened shortly before, she didn't know what to say. That seemed to be happening to her a lot lately. She hugged the book to her breast.

"I—thank you. I don't—"

"Don't say anything. Just smile for me."

Lacy was able to manage only a very watery version of a smile. If he didn't stop standing there being so endearing she didn't know what she was going to do— whether she would burst out in tears or throw herself into his arms. Either action could have just as unsettling a result.

The short distance that separated the apartment from Ariel's home seemed to be completed in the space of a heartbeat; the generous gift Sloan had given her rested with unnatural heaviness on Lacy's lap. She still couldn't comprehend why he had done it. Today had really been the first day they had actually talked. Before, they had either been snapping at each other's throats or reveling in a passionate need. Had the situation suddenly changed?

Lacy stared with uncomprehending vision out the window into the darkness. What exactly did she feel about him? Physically, she knew she was attracted to him. No, more than attracted. But was something else—another ingredient, a catalyst?—slowly being added to the determination?

Only when the Jeep drew to a stop in the driveway and the emergency brake was applied did Lacy realize that the journey was over. She turned her head in time to see that Sloan was leaving the car. She waited until he came around to her side to open the door. Then, grasping the book, she descended as well.

The following closure of the Jeep's door seemed loud in the night air, just as their footsteps did. Had today been a mere twenty-four hours? It seemed much longer than that. They had traveled approximately two hundred miles, climbed two separate—if small—mountains, eaten two meals, then visited his apartment. Was it possible that they had somehow managed to place an extra few hours into the prescribed space of time allowed in a day?

Sloan's fingers on her arm burned so intensely that Lacy almost cried out. But it was an exquisite kind of pain, so she did nothing to make them fall away. She didn't want the time to end.

The beautiful greenery that Lacy had so faithfully been watering each day was a perfect backdrop for their parting. Fronds from a fern spread their feathery leaves in front of the entryway porch, making it private from the street.

Lacy hesitated a moment after releasing the latch, her blood running rapidly through her veins. What should she do? Since the game plan seemed to have changed in midplay, did the players continue with actions from the past? Or did they make up new strategies? She was at a loss, her brain refusing to concentrate on anything other than his nearness. A tingling expectancy gripped her body.

Sloan tightened his hold, pulling her around. He took the book from her tight grasp to place it on a brick retainer. For long moments afterward he did nothing more than look at her, the half-light from the lamp left switched on in the living room casting its muted glow onto the porch. Her hazel eyes with their ring of long dark lashes were gazing up at him with a mixture of emotions swimming in their depths. Some of her hair had escaped from the captivity of the upswept knot and was moving softly against her neck in the cool night breeze. Her lips were slightly parted with unconscious seductive appeal.

He gave a muffled moan. He could stand it no longer. During the entire day he had been on his best behavior, not wanting to come on too strongly, wanting them to have time to get to know each other more, ignoring the growing desire that each passing second seemed to increase, suppressing every urge. Now the bonds he had inflicted on himself could exert their force no longer. He had to kiss her. Touch her. It was as if his very life depended on it.

Lacy's heart gave an accelerated series of jumps as

she heard the soft groan, as she saw the smoldering glimmer in his eyes when he lowered his head. She waited breathlessly for his lips to come in contact with her own. When they met, all life around them seemed to cease. Nothing else existed except themselves and the incredible sensations that were causing tongues of liquid flame to erupt and burn a rapid path through their bodies, the molten heat fusing them into one creature with one all-consuming need.

Lacy lost all sense of confusion as to what her next step should be. She pressed her slender body against his, feeling the straining muscles of his chest and thighs, glorying in the increasing masculine hardness that was crushed against her hips. When his hands roved over her back, pulling her even closer, she obliged, her lips parting, welcoming the thrust of his tongue.

The thin straps of her dress were no obstacle to further nearness. One deft flick on each and they were gone, lowered so that his questing fingertips could search for and find the burgeoning flesh.

She arched her back a degree to make his explorations less difficult, helping to dispose of the rest of her bodice until it rested in a fold at her waist.

When his fingers ran along the smooth curves, she couldn't prevent a spontaneous shiver. Like twin peaks her nipples grew taut and firm, signaling her more complete arousal.

Sloan was quick to notice the change. His palms covered the thrusting buds and teased them, making them even harder.

Lacy uttered a soft moan in response, her breaths short, quick inhalations of air. She raised her arms from their position on his shoulders and ran her fingers through his hair, enjoying the silky texture, the intimate touch. But soon that wasn't enough. She wanted to experience the sensation more fully, to touch his body, to feel the hardness and warmth of his skin.

Her fingers moved to his neck, smoothing, rubbing. Then that wasn't enough. She began to release the upper buttons of his shirt, glad that at the apartment he had discarded his jacket and tie. Within two seconds the buttons were undone.

The soft hair on his chest tickled her oversensitized fingertips at first. It was as light as the hair on his head and curled naturally as well. Lacy pressed her lips to the hard muscles.

Her action forced Sloan almost past the point of no return. He curved his body over hers, his mouth tracing the erratic pulse beneath the satin skin of her neck. When she raised her head once again, his lips strayed lower while his hands massaged the curves of her hips.

His mind sang. The bursting need could no longer be denied! It was silly to wait. She wanted him. He wanted her. Why stop? The seclusion of the house was just inches away.

For a moment Lacy thought she was going to die. Was that what it was like to love? To want someone so badly that life itself didn't seem to matter anymore? To become lost in him, never wanting to be found again if it meant a cessation of this magnificent pleasure?

Then some small spark of common sense pushed its ugly way into her consciousness. It was too soon. It was still too soon.

Her hesitation was slight, yet Sloan picked up on it and lifted his head.

His eyes, which seemed to hold heaven for the asking, looked down at her.

"Lacy?" His voice was thick, puzzled.

She was trembling, now that the full realization of how far things had gone was filtering through to her consciousness. She took a step back and began to tug at her bodice. But her fingers were clumsy and Sloan's assistance was needed.

It was very hard to cover the beauty of her breasts. Sloan did so most unwillingly. Yet she seemed intent, and he retained enough control not to force her to yield to him. He knew it would take little effort. But, again, that wasn't his way. She had to want complete sexual fulfillment as much as he. And if now wasn't the time—well, he could wait. It would be hard, but he could do it. Strangely, he was beginning to feel a protectiveness for her.

Once the upper part of her body was covered, Lacy gained a measure of surface calm. She was shaken, but she wasn't shocked by her behavior. Not at all. What was upsetting her most was this new, warm, exquisitely tender feeling for Sloan. She gave a nervous laugh. She couldn't help it. It just escaped.

Sloan expelled a deep breath, some of the tension leaving. "What a way to end a day!" he murmured facetiously.

Lacy laughed again, only this time with a little more genuineness.

He took her hand, her fingers now cold in his grasp, where only a moment before they had been heated.

"I'd like to see you tomorrow."

The remaining vocal fuzziness that showed he was still affected by what had transpired made Lacy's throat tighten. It might not be wise to accept, but she was tired of being wise. She wanted to see him, too, so she would.

"All right," she agreed.

Sloan gently squeezed her fingers. "I have to work all day, but after five I'm free. What would you like to do?"

She wondered how he would react if she told him truthfully. He certainly wouldn't want to wait until tomorrow night!

"I don't care," she replied as casually as she could.

"You're easy to please."

Lacy lifted a shoulder.

Sloan's gaze swept her, the gleam in his eyes a mixture of remaining arousal and happiness. She had agreed to see him again without hesitation.

"Tell you what. I'll call you tomorrow and we can decide then. Is that OK with you?"

She nodded and Sloan began to move away. Then he paused and came back to her, the smile on his handsome face a slow, provocative, sensual movement of well-drawn lips.

"We seem to have forgotten something," he murmured mysteriously.

Lacy's fascinated gaze never left him as he retrieved the book from the spot where he had placed it and once again gave it into her possession.

"This shouldn't be left outside all night," he explained. He followed that mild statement by leaning forward and giving her a short, sweet kiss.

"I'll see you tomorrow," he whispered. His tone was full of unspoken promise.

An unusual glitter made clear sight difficult, yet Lacy

watched his progress as he walked back to the Jeep. It might have been a reflection of the stars that populated the nighttime sky. Or it might have been something else, like the catalyst she had earlier wondered about.

Chapter Nine

Lacy spent the first hour in bed that night lying perfectly still and staring at the ceiling. Sampson was asleep at her side, his world once again at peace as soon as she had taken him into the backyard for his nightly excursion, and loved him a bit on their return. She wished everything could be so simple in her life.

She gave a deep sigh and threw one arm above her head to curve along the pillow. She refused to allow herself to sleep until she had confronted the root of her problem. Maybe it was the researcher in her, but a hanging hypothesis was anathema to her, especially now when she felt perched on the edge of some sort of dramatic breakthrough.

The growing excitement that had stolen possession of her body from the moment she had shut the door after Sloan's departure was still present. There was a new sense of life about her—almost an awakening. What was it? Colors were richer, smells were more intense, a song seemed constantly to be on the tip of her tongue, just waiting for her to discover it. Several times she had even found herself smiling when there was absolutely no cause for the action. What was happening to her?

She shifted in the bed and glanced at the clock. Yes, it was well after twelve, twelve-thirty to be exact. What was Sloan doing now? Was he asleep? Or was he lying in his bed with the same sense of excitement as she?

The thought of his long body stretched out on a sheet made Lacy's blood race. Vividly she could remember the feel of his skin, the soft golden hairs that grew on his chest. She wondered how far down they went.

Lacy could lie still no longer. She rolled onto her stomach and then flipped back onto her side, her movements exposing a great deal of flesh from beneath her gown. She gazed at the illuminated face of the clock but did not see it.

Sloan. Sloan Adams. She liked the name. She liked him! She thought about him as she had seen him on Enchanted Rock when he was resting at her side, remembered how she had wanted to reach out and run her fingers through his hair, how she had wanted to lean forward and kiss his perfect lips. Which she had, eventually. And it was everything she could have hoped.

Suddenly Lacy held her breath. She had never felt such an urge with Richard or experienced such happiness. She had worshiped him as a supplicant worships a master. She had felt pride and happiness of sorts, but it had been a much different kind of happiness. It had hinged on being given his approval. He had been a hard taskmaster, but she had loved him from the first moment she had seen him.

Or had she? The stark question asserted itself aggressively.

Lacy released her pent-up breath slowly and tried

hard to remember what Richard looked like. It had been so long since she had been able to. She concentrated fully and was rewarded with an image that could have been that of a partial stranger.

Had his eyes always been that narrowed? His hairline so receding? His mouth so determinedly set? Had the wrinkles time had brought to his fifty-three-year-old countenance always been so evident?

She examined the picture in her mind with intense interest. Yes, it was Richard. But it was a man she didn't know. It was almost as if she were seeing him for the first time.

It was irrelevant to her that he was showing signs of age. If she loved him she wouldn't care. But it was the lack of emotion she experienced that made her wonder at her true feelings. Oh, there was a certain fondness— a respect. But there was no surge of tenderness. No tingling awareness.

Was it possible that her love for Richard had been part of a monstrous game her mind had played on her? Could it have gone on for so many years? Was it Richard's dedication to his work and his unavailability because of his wife's refusal to give him a divorce that made him seem safe for her to love? Had he been an outlet for a fear she hadn't known she possessed, a fear that had kept her from opening herself to a more normal relationship? And if so, what had caused that fear? Was it a remnant from her past? Lacy frowned. She had always been sensitive to rejection, turning to books because they never closed themselves away. They were always there to be consumed. They didn't consider her some kind of freak because of her intelligence, as so many of her friends did, even though they tried not to let it show. Had that been when she had come to be afraid of having a real relationship? Had she thrown herself into her work in research, telling herself it was because of her love for Richard, only to avoid facing the truth?

Lacy turned onto her back, both arms now arced above her head, the frown creasing the skin of her forehead more pronounced. Was it possible to be so far advanced in mind yet be on the adolescent level emotionally? Yes, she answered her own question, she knew that it was. She was a perfect example. And it had taken a jolt the intensity of the highest measure on the Richter scale to prove it to her. She had to fall in love.

Lacy's heart jumped in her breast. What had she just thought? Blood began to surge through her veins and her breath came in a soft gasp. She was in love. She was in love!

A whirl of emotions swept over her: trepidation, excitement, a wild kind of joy. She was in love with Sloan Adams. And this time she knew that it was real. There was no holding back where he was concerned. Maybe that was why she had behaved so badly toward him from the first, trying to protect herself from the inevitable outcome. But it hadn't seemed to matter. She had been drawn to him by a force that wouldn't listen to logic, to timidity, to direct appeal. As if she had been a defenseless straw afloat in a stream that suddenly turned savage, she had careened toward her destiny with helpless speed.

Lacy sat up in bed, her knees drawn up against her chin, her arms hugging her legs against her breast. Sloan . . . *Oh, Sloan* — she couldn't help but wonder and hope — *Do you love me too? Is it possible that you do?*

She knew that he was forcefully attracted to her. *He* had been the one to spark their meetings in the first place and still wanted them to continue.

A happy smile spread over Lacy's soft mouth and she hugged her knees closer. If this was what it was like to really be in love, why had she waited so long? There was nothing to fear.

Sloan, too, was lying in bed, but his rest was broken by a violent thrashing about. He was asleep, yet his dream did not give him rest. He was being pursued by an unknown predator, and in his exhausted state he was unable to keep up the pace. The terror was gaining. He could feel its hot moist breath at his heels.

He awoke with a start, his body drenched in sweat, his heart pounding; the ragged breathing he was hearing was coming from his own throat. For long seconds he lay rigidly still, trying to separate reality from dream. Then his breathing slowed and his heart rate slackened off until it was more normal.

Slowly he unclenched his fists and flexed his fingers. That had been vivid! He hadn't had a dream like that in ages, not since he was a child. And then he had been the one pursuing, running after something so elusive it was never to be caught.

He rolled from his bed and made his way into the small bathroom. There he splashed water onto his face and, cupping his hands, took a drink. The water was cold and bracing, effectively destroying any remaining vestiges of the nightmare. He dried himself, then went back to the bed, collapsing on the disturbed sheets.

A psychologist would have a field day with him, he decided, folding the pillow under his head and staring

up at the darkened ceiling. Was he teetering on the
brink of paranoia, or was he just exhibiting a manifesta-
tion of extreme guilt? Sloan knew it was the latter.

How had he ever gotten himself into such a situation? Was he being repaid for some unknown offense?
Was it possible to love two women? No, not for him.
He couldn't do it. He loved only one. And the fact that
it was the wrong one was what was causing all his
troubles.

Lacy. Her name was like the most beautiful poetry to
his ears. He loved her. He probably had from the first
moment he saw her. He certainly hadn't been able to
leave her alone. Just the thought of her made his body
ache, his soul rejoice.

But what of Caroline? What would he do about Caroline? It was true they had never actually spoken of marriage. It had just been assumed. But did that make it
any less of a fact?

Sloan groaned and reclenched his fist. How could he
hurt her? Caroline's round face with its angel-like expression rose to fill his inner vision. It would be like
destroying a trusting, perfectly healthy animal only because it had outlived its usefulness to the family who
owned it. He could no more hurt her than he could the
animal. Not to mention Jim. What would his defection
do to Jim, the man who had been much more of a
father to him than had his own flesh and blood?

Sloan turned onto his side, his eyes wide open. He
stared blindly at the wall. What was he going to do?

As the morning sun made its regular appearance over
the eastern horizon, Sloan awakened. He felt much
more refreshed than he had thought possible, consider-

ing the night he had spent. Within him there was still a terrible gnawing pain, but, as well, there was a stronger sense of happiness when he thought that again tonight he was going to be with Lacy.

Luckily for him the workday was full, making the time pass quickly. Sloan took a moment midday between operations to place a quick call to Lacy. He couldn't seem to help the nervous excitement that caught hold of him as he dialed her number.

When he heard her voice, there was a curling sensation in the pit of his stomach. "Hello, Lacy? This is Sloan." There was a moment's pause. He began to wonder if they had been disconnected.

"Hello, Sloan," she returned at last. Sloan let out a silent breath.

"Did you sleep well?" What a question! Did he really expect her to answer? And if she did, was he supposed to tell her next how his night had passed?

"Yes," came her soft reply.

Sloan took himself in hand. He was behaving like a juvenile! "I told you I'd call about tonight—"

"Is there a problem?" she interrupted quickly, cutting into his words.

Was she hoping that there would be? Was she pulling away from him once again? "No," Sloan answered slowly, then more strongly, "No, not at all. I was just wanting to see what you'd like to do. I told you I'd call and we'd decide."

"Oh."

Was she disappointed? Sloan's chin firmed. "There's a place I know. It's not exactly high class, but its got a lot of flavor. The local talent tries out there: bands, singers, comedians. Usually there's enough to appreciate. We can get something to eat on the way. What do you think?"

Lacy was silent a moment. Then, "Sure, that sounds fine."

Sloan's grip tightened on the telephone. He wished he could see her now—see why she was so—well, almost cool. Did she not want to go out with him? "Yeah, well, OK. Look, I've got to go now. I'm supposed to be in surgery. I'll see you about seven."

"About seven," she repeated.

Sloan waited a moment, wondering if he should say something more. He could still hear her breathing on the other end. But he remained silent and afterward cursed himself for his foolishness.

The afternoon was almost over, the last rabies shot scheduled having been delivered into the rolling flesh of an overweight Labrador. Sloan was patting the dog's shiny black coat and telling her that she had been a good girl when Max slid his head into the examination room and, in as subdued a manner as he was able to manage, told Sloan that he had a call.

Was it Lacy? Was she canceling their plans? If she was, he would go to her house anyway.

He finished with the dog and owner and rushed to the telephone, ready with his lines of defense. He would attack, harassing her into seeing him if he had to.

The voice on the line was feminine, but it was not Lacy. It was Caroline. Sloan leaned his shoulder against the wall in relief. But his ease was not allowed for long. Immediately upon realizing that it was Caroline, his conscience twisted, and a return of the guilt he was becoming accustomed to surfaced and multiplied.

"I'm sorry to bother you so late, Sloan, but I wanted to make sure you're still coming to dinner tonight," Caroline offered brightly. "Dad is going to speak at that Chamber of Commerce meeting, so he's not going to be here. But I thought—"

Sloan castigated himself for not remembering that this was Wednesday. The fact had slipped his mind, with so many other things to think about. He broke into her words. "Caroline, listen. I can't. I'm sorry. I forgot what day today is and already made—some other plans."

"Oh? You have?" He could hear the disappointment in her voice and cursed himself with more intensity.

"If I could change them, I would. But—" He hoped she didn't ask what he was doing. He didn't want to have to lie to her. Soon the problem would have to be faced. But he wanted just another night. He had to have another night—to think.

Caroline's answer was immediate. "That's all right, Sloan. I understand." She laughed lightly. "Living with Dad lately makes me understand perfectly. Do you know, this morning he almost forgot to go into the clinic? He thought today was his day off."

Sloan laughed as well. It was easier that way. "I've been known to do that myself."

"I know," Carolline returned. "That's what I'm talking about. It's just like you're a member of the family!"

A fine perspiration broke out above Sloan's upper lip.

He was saved from coming up with some sort of reply by Caroline herself. "Whatever you're doing," she teased, "that's more important than coming over here—I hope you enjoy yourself. I'm having my special turkey Tetrazzini, with a chocolate cake for dessert."

"Sounds good."

"I can't tempt you to change your mind?"

"Sorry."

"I'll think about you when I eat your piece of cake."

He couldn't prevent a smile. She had to be so careful about her weight. "You'd better save it for me," he warned. "Every extra calorie is a pound."

Caroline made an annoyed sound deep in her throat, then laughed and hung up the phone.

Sloan disconnected from his end as well, but there was no smile in his eyes or on his lips as he walked to the rear of the building to check the animals he had earlier operated upon. Max was already in the room, and the two worked silently, efficiently. When they were finished, Max looked at Sloan through narrowed eyes, his bushy hair and beard complementing his bearish build perfectly.

"I couldn't help but overhear. I tried not to, but—"

Sloan swung around slowly. He met Max's eyes.

"And?"

Max took a deep breath only to let it out in one big whoosh. "And—if you ever want to talk, I'm available. Remember that."

Sloan absorbed the message in silence, then he gave a crooked smile and nodded. "I'll remember."

Max busied himself with a cat, and Sloan slipped out of his lab coat before leaving the building.

Lacy was ready long before Sloan was scheduled to arrive. She had already taken Sampson for his walk and checked that the special lock on the rear patio door was secured. After that there was little to do but wait—and think.

Last night, just before dropping off, she couldn't help but wonder if the revelation she had so recently discovered would stand up to the harsh light of day. Perhaps she was being imaginative; perhaps she was still reeling from his sensual spell.

But as soon as she slid from the gentle grasp of sleep, she knew her conclusion was fact. The same happy excitement enveloped her, the same good cheer that wanted—no, needed—to be shared. She felt as if she were the first woman to make such a discovery. Surely no one else had ever experienced such a glorious, glowing happiness.

Even Sampson sensed the change in her. He frolicked and played, mirroring her enjoyment of the day, until he succeeded in wearing himself out completely.

Lacy glanced down at the silver ball of rolled-up poodle that was now sleeping soundly at her feet, and an affectionate smile curved her lips. He had been her special companion of the day, making the time pass more quickly, trying to understand, in his canine way, her human peculiarities.

He had been there to get her through the minutes following Sloan's call when she had been so angry with herself because she had sounded distant, when what she had really wanted to do was tell him to drop everything and come to her right then. Sampson had watched her disgusted movements, then quietly had given her ankle a soothing lick. At that loving gesture Lacy's irritation with herself instantly evaporated and she scooped the little dog up into her arms to bury her face in his soft hair.

Now, at last, she had to deal with her emotions alone, and all she could do was wait with mounting impatience for Sloan to arrive.

At exactly seven o'clock her wait came to an end. The doorbell rang, and Lacy had to forcibly stop herself from bounding across the room to answer it. What stopped her now was what had stopped her previously during the telephone call: her unsureness of him. He wanted to be with her; he wanted to make love to her. She knew that without a doubt. But was there anything more to his feelings than that? She didn't know.

Raising her chin Lacy moved smoothly into the entryway, the soft swish of her cobalt-blue silk dress against her thighs giving her confidence. She knew she looked her best. She had had all afternoon for preparation, and she had taken special care. When she opened the door, her painstaking thoroughness was rewarded. Sloan's blue eyes widened, and it was as if he could not take his gaze away from the vision there before him.

Lacy smiled, her confidence gaining. "Sloan—come in. You're right on time."

She extended her hand and he automatically reached out to take it. He moved into the house as one who suddenly finds himself thrust into a shimmering dream. His voice was husky when at last he was able to speak.

"I told you you were beautiful once. You're not. You're breathtaking."

Lacy accepted the compliment with as much sophistication as she could muster. She tipped her head, making the shiny beauty of her chestnut hair move against her shoulders.

Sloan's rapt attention moved from her face to her

hair, then to the clinging design of the simple dress. If it had been of a different material, the dress would have been plain. But being silk and such a vibrant color, there was nothing ordinary about it. Lacy was glad she had raided Ariel's closet. They had always been the same size and often traded clothing when the need arose during their teenage years, although she had to admit that she had been the one to do most of the borrowing. She seemed never to have had anything appropriate to wear when she had accepted an occasional date. As was the case now. There had been absolutely nothing of this sort in her suitcase brought from Boston. And she knew Ariel wouldn't mind.

"Breathtaking," he repeated.

Lacy could uphold her calm exterior no longer. She felt the light blush as it rose from her neck into her cheeks. Damn! Why did she have to act so inexperienced? Because she was? a little voice returned. Lacy gave her head an imperious shake. Well, maybe that wouldn't be the case for much longer. Maybe not after tonight.

Sloan himself was no slouch. He was wearing another dark suit—this time in brown—that fit impeccably, and a subtly striped shirt in shades of tan on white. As she had speculated when she first saw him on the plane, he could have worked for a men's fashion magazine. With his Nordic good looks and excellent build he would have been perfect for the part.

She pulled her hand away, self-conscious that he was still holding it. A short silence followed her action. Then Sloan, breaking free from his trance-like state, asked if she was ready to leave.

Lacy concurred. What she really wanted to do was

stay, but she didn't see how she could tell him that without being too obvious. And she didn't know how she would handle the situation if he refused.

Before leaving though, she took a moment to talk to Sampson, bending down to stroke his head. "I'll be back, love," she promised. After all they had been through together over the last couple of weeks, and especially after today when he had been her only friend, she didn't think it appropriate to leave without acknowledging him. And if that meant she was becoming as silly as Ariel, then she guessed that she was.

Sloan's smile was her reward when she turned back to him. He seemed to approve of her consideration of Sampson's feelings.

When they were approaching the Jeep, Sloan's hand at her waist tightened. She looked up at him. "I wish I had something better to drive. A Cadillac or something. You don't look as if you should have to ride in a raunchy Renegade."

Lacy couldn't prevent a wry smile. He didn't seem the Cadillac type. It would fit his looks, but not his personality.

"The Jeep is fine," she reassured him.

Sloan looked steadily into her eyes, a warmth lighting their depths. "What makes me think you're saying that just to make me feel better?"

Lacy gave a nonchalant shrug. "Think what you will. I like the Jeep."

He helped her into her seat. "You'd refuse a Cadillac?"

She looked across at him. He was leaning forward so that he could see her easily. "I wouldn't if you were driving it."

Following that admission, a sudden wave of awareness of exactly what she had said made Lacy want to take it back. Talk about obvious. Why didn't she just come right out and ask him to take her to bed!

Sloan held himself rigid. Had he heard her correctly? He looked deeply into her eyes and saw that he had. They showed consternation mixed with a growing determination, as well as something else he could not identify. His heart gave a surprised leap.

A tension like none they had ever experienced before sprang up between them. In the past there had always been a tremendous sexual awareness. It was still there now, magnified many times over; but there was another ingredient as well—something that was in each of them—something that was hovering on the edge of disclosure. Something tangible, something real.

A powerful fist could have hit Sloan directly in the midsection, so hard did he find it to speak. He didn't want to say the wrong thing.

"Do you really want to go to the club?"

Lacy's stomach plunged. She searched his face for some sign of emotion. For the first time it was closed to her. She answered honestly.

"No."

Sloan's grip on the door and roof tightened. "Then let's not." His hesitation was only slight. "Let's go to my place instead."

If the electricity generated by those words could have been harnessed by the city power company, the citizens of Austin would not have had to worry about the interruption of service for at least a thousand years.

Lacy swallowed. She knew what would happen if they did. Was she ready this time? Before, she had not been. But now, knowing that she loved him—and looking at him she could only admit that her love was increasing—she could no longer deny what both her heart and her body wanted. She had to grow up sometime. If he wanted her he could have her. She felt enough love for both of them.

"Yes." Her quiet answer held resolution.

Sloan heard the whispered word, and the ache in his groin that had begun the first second he saw her looking so stunningly lovely this evening became an active pain. The throbbing was unremittant. He gave no reply, but the heat from his gaze raking over her spoke for itself.

His apartment was just the same as Lacy remembered it. But since only one day had passed since her presence there, she couldn't really have expected it to change.

As far as Sloan was concerned, he wanted to take her directly into his bedroom. Forget finesse; to hell with all the games that led up to seduction. But something held him back. Was it Lacy's own hesitation? Had she changed her mind again?

He watched her carefully as she moved about the room, restlessly touching a wooden African face mask that was placed on a shelf, studying the Monet print once again, coming behind the couch and running a finger down the length of its back, stopping to examine a figurine.

She couldn't stay still. Why was he just looking at her? He had brought her here for a reason, hadn't he? He hadn't done it just for decoration.

Sloan caught her hand as she moved in front of him, intent on another sweep of the room.

"Do you want to leave?" he asked softly.

That question had a familiar ring to it. He had asked that of her before. A second passed. "No."

His gaze held her own as he warned, "Both people have to want it for it to be right."

She didn't ask to what he was referring. "I know."

"And?"

Lacy's cheeks took on some color, but she held her chin up high. For an answer she placed her hands on his shoulders and raised up on tiptoe, placing her lips tentatively against his.

At first Sloan gave no reaction. He held her arms in his tight grasp and let her do all the work of continuing the kiss. Then all at once there was a change. The fires that had been steadily building within him for much too long a time slipped their inhibiting restraints and burst into a raging inferno of flaming need. Mindful only of this need he crushed her body to his.

Melded to him as she was, Lacy was breathlessly aware of the outline of his hard masculine frame as it imprinted itself upon her. A rush of desire spread through her, radiating from her core to her fingertips as she smoothed her hands down across the strong muscles of his back, feeling through the jacket of his suit the way they were moving as he strained her close.

Then Sloan was pulling his mouth away, but it was only long enough to discard the coat, to throw his tie on the couch behind them as well. Instantly his mouth came back to cover hers with even more intensity than it had before.

Lacy's lips parted under the direct assault and soon his tongue was tasting the sweetness of the interior of her mouth. Lacy gave a soft, acquiescent moan and let the tip of her tongue engage in a sweet duel with his.

Sloan's breathing was ragged when he pulled away, his eyes glittering with intensity. His hands were at her ribs, his thumbs brushing the side curves of her throbbing breasts.

"I want you, Lacy," he stated roughly.

Without hesitation Lacy gave the answer he required. "I want you, too." Her body was alive with feeling.

The blue of Sloan's eyes shone with vivid intensity. "I don't want to wait any more."

Was he giving her another opportunity to change her mind? Deliberately Lacy trailed her fingers across his chest to the buttons of his shirt. There she undid one and slid her hand inside to feel the warmth. Her pleasure heightened at the boldness of her action. "Neither do I."

For Sloan there was no turning back. He wanted her as he had never wanted another woman. He bent and scooped her from her feet, one arm supporting her legs at the knees. He walked into his bedroom and placed her on the bed.

How often lately had he dreamed of doing this very thing? Yet somehow it didn't seem real. Could it be just another fantasy he was acting out in his mind? He began to tremble, afraid to move as he continued to stare down at her.

Lacy's entire being was caught up in the moment. She waited as he stood beside her, his blond hair falling down over his forehead in disarray. He was so handsome! Did he know he was driving her crazy? She reached out for him, not wanting their separation to continue.

Sloan delayed no longer. If this was a dream he would willingly enter its realm. But as soon as he touched her, he knew that no fantasy could duplicate the sweet smoothness of her skin; no imagined pleasure could come close to matching the reality of her lips.

Sloan wanted this moment to go on forever, but the increasing demands of his body would not allow for a long preamble. He slid the zipper of her dress down and then gently freed her arms. The slip and bra beneath soon followed.

Lacy helped as much as she was able. She wasn't practiced in the subtle art, but she was a quick learner. When all that remained were her lace panties, she stopped him as he started to remove these as well.

His gaze met her hazel eyes. In them he read no shame; he saw only a heated glow. For a space of seconds he was puzzled; then, as she began to unbutton the rest of his shirt he understood. He held his breath as her fingers worked, stroking his skin, exploring the finely haired area of his chest, seemingly delighting in their discoveries. Yet, soon her hands lowered and she held her bottom lip as she unbuckled his belt.

Lacy could barely breathe. She was amazed at her brazenness. Yet she couldn't stop. She was being driven on by something she couldn't control. With some clumsiness she released the catch and short zipper, aware with heightened senses of the hard masculine protuberance that was so very close to her touch. but it was there that shyness and innocence asserted themselves and she could go no further.

Somewhere in the blaze that was consuming him Sloan reflected on her hesitation. He waited for her to continue, the unstinting heat of his passion holding him firmly in its grip. When she remained still, he finished the task for her, ridding himself of slacks and briefs and shirt with quick movements.

Lacy gave a startled gasp as she felt his nude body rise to cover hers, felt his fingers pulling to lower her panties. He took her gasp as a sign of pleasure, the pounding in his ears making every sound come as if it were softer.

She had only a moment to become adapted to the unaccustomed touch of his skin before she had to deal with a thousand other sensations as his hand ran up and down her body, over the curve of her hip, along her waist, cupping her breast—reveling in the softness—teasing her nipple. Then it grazed the flatness of her stomach and continued lower. There his fingers began an exploratory foray in an area she had never before allowed a man to touch. For an instant Lacy stiffened, then as the touch became more familiar, a growing pleasure like none she had ever experienced kept her from issuing a protest.

Sloan's lips were on her throat, burying themselves in the sensitive hollow at its base, his tongue marking the rapid pulse. But soon his head moved, transferring to the glorious softness that only a moment before had known his touch. His lips at her breast made Lacy arch, the combined pleasures almost too much for her. Her fingers dug into his back.

Sloan reacted as a man possessed. He stopped all form of touching and braced himself on his arms while positioning his hips to best advantage between her yielding legs.

When Lacy felt the first thrust of the rite of initiation, she again gave an unconcious gasp. This time, though, it was something more than fear and awe. It was delight. She had always thought it would hurt a little. But it hadn't. Had she been told wrong? Or was it just a quirk of her makeup?

The bodily fullness that soon followed was strange in the beginning, then as she allowed herself to relax, her enjoyment began to increase until she was at almost the same level of excitement as Sloan. The thrusting continued and heightened in intensity.

Sloan tried to last. Being a part of her was paradise! But it had been so long since he had had a woman. With a shuddering moan that came from deep within him, he gave himself over to the delicious, indescribable sensations of release.

When finally he was still, lying against her, yet keeping his full weight from crushing her, Lacy experienced joy. She had liked what had happened. Liked it a lot. She was glad she had done it, glad she had waited for Sloan. She didn't want to share a closeness of this sort with anyone else.

After a time he raised his body and rolled over onto his side, hugging her to him. He pressed her head into the curve of his shoulder, his fingers threaded in her hair, and stared up at the ceiling, waiting for his heart to subside to some kind of normalcy. He loved her. He loved her totally, completely! He had made love to women before, but never had he had this kind of satisfaction.

He slowly released her head and allowed her the freedom to move. When she looked up at him with those wide hazel eyes it was all he could to not to start kissing her again. Instead, he apologized.

"I'm sorry you didn't get a lot out of that." His smile was wry. "I'm out of practice, I guess. Either that or you excite the hell out of me. I think it's a bit of both."

Lacy was unsure of what he meant. She had enjoyed what had occurred between them. She hurried to reassure him. "I enjoyed it."

He disagreed. "But not as much as you could have. I came too soon. Next time it will be better for you. I'll see that it is."

Lacy remained quiet. She didn't want to contradict him again. And if he was promising more, she was ready to wait to see the mystery unraveled. She burrowed close to him.

Absently Sloan's fingers began to play in the long strands of her hair, raising some up and then letting them slide through.

He turned and gave a soft kiss to the top of her head. He felt he had to tell her. "You know something?" he whispered huskily. Lacy tried to raise up to look at him, but he kept her still. "I think I'm falling in love with you."

Those words could have been a golden coin falling into a paper-thin bowl of the finest crystal for all the impact they had. They shattered into Lacy's soul. They made the act complete. He loved her. He loved her as she loved him!

She was opening her lips in preparation of telling him her secret when the jangling of the telephone next to the bed cut into the silence and caused them both to jump.

Sloan gave a soft laugh and Lacy gave one in return, amusement at their mutual start weaving another thread of closeness into the blanket that might one day cover them with happiness.

On the second ring Sloan leaned over to answer the phone, a surge of joy still echoing in his voice as he gave acknowledgement.

But as he listened to the person on the other end of the line, all the happiness of the moment before left his expression, and his face seemed to freeze. "Now, wait. Calm down. Tell me again. How is he?" He was silent a moment.

Lacy placed a hand on his arm, sensing his disturbance.

He seemed not to notice. "Where is he now?" He repeated the name of a hospital in Austin. "OK, Caroline. Just stay where you are. I'll come get you."

More troubled conversation came across the line. Lacy cold hear the feminine voice, and a sinking sensation made her feel almost sick. Caroline? Who was Caroline? And what was she to Sloan?

"I'll be right there," Sloan said firmly, and swinging his feet to the floor, he caused Lacy's hand to fall away. He settled the receiver back onto its hook and ran a hand through his hair, disturbing it even more. Automatically he began to search for his clothing.

Lacy sat upright, pulling the sheet upward to cover her. She felt all funny inside, as if something special had been within her grasp and was now suddenly in danger of slipping away. She felt as if she had to capture it now or it might forever be lost.

"Is something wrong?" she found voice enough to ask.

Sloan paused in pulling on his slacks. He glanced at her, at the beautiful picture she made in his bed. His

heart jolted. How could he explain? He had wanted to
tell her carefully, slowly. He couldn't possibly do it
now. Not now.

"A friend of mine is in the hospital. They think he
might have had a stroke."

"A stroke?"

He nodded, settling the slacks on his hips.

Lacy gathered nerve from somewhere.

"Who is Caroline?" *Oh, please, let it be the man's
wife!*

"His daughter."

Lacy absorbed the shock, her face losing some color.

"Is she a friend of yours, too?" She couldn't help it.
She knew at this time she shouldn't be bitchy. He
needed to leave. But she couldn't seem to stop herself.
She had to know.

"Yes."

She said no more. Sloan eyed her from across the
room where he had moved to get his shirt. He had
really tossed it away in his hurry earlier. He saw her
hurt expression, but knew nothing could be done about
it now. Except: "I've known her since we were both
children."

Lacy took it the way he wanted her to for that moment. She looked relieved.

"Can I do anything to help?" she offered, meaning
it. If something affected Sloan it affected her.

"You can get dressed," Sloan returned, softening his
words with a slight grin as he tucked in his shirt and,
after reattaching his pants clasp, zipped his fly.

She blinked. "Oh!" She had forgotten where she was.

"I don't know how long I'll be—possibly the rest of
the night. I don't know."

Lacy was immediately repentant. She castigated herself for her selfishness. She had barely given a thought to the stricken man.

"I'll be ready in two minutes." With uninhibited grace she hopped from the bed and began a hurried reapplication of her clothing.

The drive back to Ariel's was short and fast, Sloan not minding the speed zones very carefully. If Lacy had speculated for a thousand years she would never have thought that the night would end in this manner. Still, she had the feeling that something important was missing, something to do with the call. But she couldn't put a name to it and didn't want to bother Sloan. He was worried enough already.

When he saw her to her door, he stayed only long enough to give her a swift kiss before dashing back to the Renegade and speeding off into the night.

Lacy let herself into the house. So much had changed. In fact, everything had changed. She had loved a man and been loved by him in return. He had even told her that he was falling in love with her. But the hollow ache that had started earlier would not go away. In fact, as the moon crossed the sky and disappeared behind the horizon to be replaced by the sun, the hurt had begun to assume monumental proportions. Worry, a newfound jealousy, and love all mingled together to make her a wholly miserable wretch.

Chapter Ten

Caroline collapsed into Sloan's arms as soon as she allowed him to enter her home. It was as if she had been waiting for his arrival to dissolve into tears.

Sloan drew her to him, sharing her sorrow. But even at this moment, he couldn't forget the woman he had so recently held. Lacy was taller, more slender. The curves of her body were less pronounced. And because of what had so recently passed between them, he felt uneasy offering protection to another.

Yet when Caroline gulped and started to apologize, wiping at her nose with a balled-up tissue, looking so much like the little girl he remembered from his childhood, his conscience immediately began to assail him. Yes, he loved Lacy. What he felt for her was without question. But Caroline didn't know that. She had no inkling. And there was no way he could possibly begin to tell her now.

Sloan pulled a handkerchief from his pocket and offered it to her, his gaze filled with concern. Caroline needed him, needed him as she had at no time in the past. He couldn't let her down. Neither could he worry about his future actions concerning Lacy. What he had to do at this moment was help his friends. His wishes and desires had to be postponed. He pressed Caroline close against him, hoping that some of his strength could be shared.

When at last she composed herself, Caroline straightened a measure away. She didn't break their physical connection completely; it was as if she didn't trust herself not to cave in to her turbulent emotions again if she did.

"Can you tell me a little more about what happened?" Sloan questioned, tenderly pushing some blond strands of hair away from her moist cheeks.

"All I know is what I told you," Caroline whispered brokenly. "Donald Clements called me. He's the man who invited Dad to speak at the dinner. He told me Dad had collapsed. He—he said a doctor there thought it looked like a stroke." Caroline sniffed and strove to keep control of her voice. "I called you right after that." She looked up at him, her big blue eyes filled with tears. "I'm sorry I interrupted your evening. The only thing I could think of was to tell you."

"It's all right," Sloan assured her. "I'm glad you did."

Caroline sniffed again. "I didn't take you away from anything special, did I? I was worried because of what you said earlier, about not coming here."

A dark wave of regret swept through Sloan as he was forced into a lie. "No," he returned evenly, flatly, "you didn't interrupt anything." How could he stand there and say that so calmly? He was beginning to hate himself.

Caroline gave a deep, relieved sigh. "I'm glad."

He collected himself once again. Right now, first

things had to be taken care of first. "Are you ready to go? We should learn more at the hospital. Has your father's own doctor been notified?"

A look of dismay appeared on Caroline's face. "I don't know. I didn't think—"

Sloan brushed her concern away. "Don't worry about it. I'm sure he's been called by now."

Caroline moved with him toward the door. "Oh, I hope so. I never thought—all I could do was call you."

Sloan's arm tightened about her. He said nothing, but the depth of her reliance stung him deeply.

The next eight hours were some of the hardest Sloan had ever spent. The hospital waiting room was cold and unfriendly and smelled of stale cigarette smoke. The television attached high up on one wall was switched off for the night, and the outdated magazines meant to help pass time were all ragged and torn from a succession of too many nervous fingers. Tasteless coffee from a nearby machine was the only beverage available to sustain them.

Sloan checked his watch as the first rays of morning light tried to make their way through a dust-encrusted skylight above them. It was almost six o'clock. He stretched and yawned, rubbing the fingers of one hand over the light stubble of beard that had grown there overnight. Caroline was asleep in the chair next to him, curled into as comfortable a position as she could manage.

His heart melted at the sight. She looked so young. Much younger than her twenty-nine years. She could have been closer to nineteen. She had not wanted to go to sleep, but he had encouraged her, telling her that he would wake her if there was any news.

His movements must have disturbed her, because Caroline began to awaken. Sloan gave a small smile and welcomed, "Hi, sleepyhead."

At first Caroline didn't seem to understand where she was, then her eyes took on a look of remembered fear and she straightened quickly. "What's happened? Has anything happened?"

Sloan shook his head. "Nothing. Not a thing."

Some of the tautness left her body. She fell back against the hard rear cushion of the chair. "Did I sleep long?"

"Not very."

"No one's come in?"

"The doctor did about an hour ago. But nothing has changed."

"You didn't wake me!" It was almost an accusation.

"No."

"You told me you would."

"If there had been anything to tell you, I would. But there wasn't, so I let you sleep. I figured you needed it."

Caroline looked as if she was about to form another protest, then the fight left her. She slumped even more into her chair. Finally she breathed, "Yes, I suppose you were right. I don't know what I'd do without you, Sloan," before letting her eyelids flutter shut once again.

Her words pierced his soul. Sloan looked from Caroline to the drably painted wall he had been studying for so long and released a deep, painful sigh.

An hour later, he was on his way home. The doctor had finally come with some encouraging news—Jim's stroke had been a light one—and Caroline had rushed in to be with her father, deciding to stay with him while Sloan went home to get some sleep.

His rest could only be for a small period, however, because with Jim unable to handle his share of the work for today as well as for some time to come, both he and Max were going to have to stretch their hours considerably.

But as he drove out of the city and onto the street leading into the subdivision, an instinctive homing sense made him pass the entry to his apartment and drive on until he came to Willow Street.

Lacy greeted his arrival as if she had been waiting for him.

"Well, how is he?" she asked, following his steps into the living room and pausing at his side as he dropped onto the sofa.

"He'll make it." Sloan rubbed his aching forehead.

Lacy's eyes traveled over him. He was still wearing the brown slacks and tan and white shirt that he had hurried back into last night. But now he didn't look like any kind of men's model, unless the client wanted one who gave the impression that lifting a toothpick was a tremendous chore. Her instincts told her to question him further. Too much of her time during the nighttime hours had been spent on speculation, especially about the mysterious Caroline. But common sense told her that now was not the time. She buried her curiosity under the cover of concern.

"You look exhausted."

"I am."

"Have you eaten anything this morning?"

"No."

"Then let me fix you something." She started toward the kitchen, but Sloan's voice stopped her before she could leave the room. He asked if he could use the telephone.

"Sure," she replied, glancing back over her shoulder.

"I have to let Max know what's happened.' He glanced about the room. "Where is it?"

"There's one in here." Lacy motioned to the kitchen where she was headed. "And one in any of the bedrooms down the hall. Ariel and David have a telephone in just about every room of the house except the living room. Don't ask me why there's not one there too. All I can tell you is that there isn't."

She watched as Sloan pushed heavily to his feet, looking as if he were about to pass out where he stood. He made no reply as he moved in the direction of the hall.

From the kitchen, Lacy soon heard the sound of Sampson's usual happy barking on seeing the vet and knew that Sloan had picked the phone in her bedroom to make his call. That thought forced a gaggle of goose bumps to break out on her skin.

Ten minutes later Lacy made her way back into the living room, carrying a tray containing two freshly fried eggs, four brown-and-serve sausages, and a piece of buttered toast. She had no idea what Sloan liked to eat, but she decided the usual all-American breakfast wouldn't be far off the mark.

The living room was empty when she entered it.

"Sloan?" she called into the empty air. She walked into the hall and called softly again. Was he still using the telephone? She rounded the corner of her bedroom and stopped short. Sloan was still there, all right, but he was now stretched out fully on her bed—asleep, the poodle lying at his side as if guarding him.

Lacy's grasp on the tray slackened. Now what should she do? Should she awaken him or should she leave him there? She decided that he obviously needed sleep more than food, so with great care she left the room—although the way he was sleeping she could have been an entire herd of elephants charging through and he wouldn't have known. She made her way back into the kitchen, Sampson at her heels—the dog having changed allegiance at the scent of food—and sat down at the small round table to eat part of the breakfast herself. She had been much too upset to eat anything earlier, but now that he was here, a little of the unsettled jealousy she had experienced earlier—he had come back to *her*—had dissipated enough to let the inviting aromas rising from the plate tempt her. She could resist no longer and enjoyed the breakfast much more than she had enjoyed any meal in a long time. Then, when memory told her that she had skipped her evening meal the night before, she understood why she was so hungry.

Sloan remained asleep for most of the morning. Lacy checked on him occasionally, but each time she did, she saw that he had moved barely at all. He appeared to be sleeping the sleep of the dead. Finally, during one of her visits, he stirred.

A part of her wanted to hurry away so that he wouldn't see she had been watching him. But another part of her wouldn't let her move. She remained where she was.

Sloan awakened with a start. He didn't know where

he was. Then, as his questioning gaze came to rest on Lacy, he relaxed and turned onto his side, his head balanced on his raised palm. A warm light started in the depths of his eyes, and a slow smile tilted his lips, making the lines in his cheeks deepen.

"I didn't know heaven made special deliveries," he murmured softly.

Lacy felt the jolt of his appreciative look all the way to her toes. It made her extremely conscious that her white jeans and jade green cotton shirt fitted her snugly. Yet she retained a surface calm, resisting the melting feeling that made her muscles become weak.

"I wouldn't count on the fact that this is heaven, if I were you. The way you were sleeping, the devil himself could have crept in to leave a surprise and you wouldn't have known it."

"You?" he countered immediately.

"No, the courage to use that corny line."

His smile increased. "You didn't like it?"

Lacy tipped her head. It was all she could do not to run across the room and jump into bed with him. "Well, on a scale of one to ten, that was definitely sub-zero."

Sloan pretended to be wounded. "I can see I'll have to get in some practice." He paused. "I have an idea. Why don't you come over here a little closer and let me start over again." He patted the bed at his side. "Come on. I do my best work in close quarters."

There was nothing Lacy would rather do, but she continued to hold back. "Aren't you hungry? You were practically starving earlier."

"That depends upon what kind of food you're referring to: food for the soul or for the body."

"I believe I meant for the body."

"Then what are we waiting for?" He held out his hand. Either answer would have received the same reply.

Lacy's knees began to tremble. She knew she should question him more closely about Caroline, about the degree of their friendship. But at this particular moment she purposely chose not to let the name or the person get in the way. If there was a problem, she would deal with it later. Right now there was a more demanding situation that needed to be seen to.

Lacy crossed the room, all the while keeping Sloan's gaze a captive of her own. Had it only been last night that they were together? In some ways, remembering what it felt like to lie next to him, to have him touch her, to have him possess her—it had been much too long a time. And yet in other ways—there might not have been any interruption. This could be a continuation of what had preceeded just moments before.

Her knee was resting on the bed, his hand was gripping hers, his eyes were glittering with sensual enjoyment and expectation, when once again the telephone cut into the heavily charged atmosphere between them. Only this time neither jumped; this time both were so caught up in love's potent spell that they barely heard.

It rang three times before Sloan frowned and glanced about the room trying to trace the sound. Reality was filtering through to a mind that was intent on ignoring the difficulties ahead. If he had awakened alone he would have been all right. He might have gotten up, spoken quietly with Lacy in the kitchen or wherever she was, and then left, at all times keeping himself under strong control. But when he turned and saw her standing there, looking both so beautiful and desirable, nothing else seemed to matter but her. He wanted to be close to her again, to feel her lying pressed against him. He needed the warmth and assurance that only she could give.

The telephone rang again, and this time Lacy heard it. The two of them looked deeply at each other for several long seconds: then, before it could ring once more, Lacy answered.

Her voice was tight, not sounding at all like her own. She tried to clear her throat, but the act did no good.

"Hello—"

"Hello? Is this—?" Ariel's phone number was quoted.

"Yes, yes it is." Lacy's grip on the receiver was uncertain. Sloan's hand was now at her waist and she was extremely conscious of his touch. There was a small silence. Then Lacy asked, "Who is this, please?" when what she really wanted to do was to scream at whoever was on the line to leave them alone.

The feminine voice came again. It did not answer the question, but instead asked one of its own. "Is Sloan Adams there?"

Lacy experienced a stab of returning jealousy. Was this the person who had interrupted them last night? Was it Caroline? She was coming to despise the name. She held her ground. "Who may I say is calling?"

"This is Mrs. Steinbeck, the office manager at Twin Oaks Veterinary Hospital. Dr. Max Dalton asked me to contact Dr. Adams. Please put me through."

Some of the tenseness that had come to take hold of Lacy's body left, and a feeling of foolishness took its place. She motioned Sloan to the telephone.

"For you."

He took the receiver, using the hand that had been at her waist. "Yes?" he spoke into the mouthpiece.

Mrs. Steinbeck answered; Lacy could hear the drone of her words. Her side felt naked without Sloan's touch.

"Yes," Sloan repeated, only this time with more decisiveness. "Tell Max I'm on my way." A hasty glance at his watch had him swinging his legs from the bed. "I didn't mean to be this long." He muttered the last words more to himself than to the woman on the line. But she must have heard and given some kind of comment because a slow, dull red stole up Sloan's neck. Lacy could see his flash of irritation before he replied shortly, "I don't consider what I do with my time any business of yours, Mrs. Steinbeck. So kindly keep your opinions to yourself. Either that or find yourself another job."

Without waiting for a reply, Sloan slammed the receiver down on its stand. He had taken about all he was going to from Mrs. Steinbeck. Just because she considered herself a moralist she had no right to impose her views on someone else, especially on him. He was already having enough trouble all by himself, thank you. He didn't need her waspish words to add more.

Lacy watched as Sloan stood up and began to tuck his shirt back into the waistband of his pants. His irritation was still evident in the efficient way he moved. He looked around for his shoes and, finding them, slipped first one foot and then the other into its leather cover. Several seconds passed before he glanced at her, and when he did, he was still dealing with the aftereffects of his anger. Yet it wasn't her fault; none of this was her fault. He knew it was his own inability to master the fates that made him feel so impotent.

Lacy saw his anger and wondered at its cause. She knew he was upset with the caller, but there seemed to be something more.

"Should I have awakened you earlier? I didn't know. You looked so tired."

Sloan's gaze struck Lacy's puzzled hazel eyes and immediately all his anger dissolved. He could be disgusted with himself all he wanted—and Lord knew he had reason. But to take his problems out on Lacy was criminal, even if she was the root cause.

He rolled the muscles of his shoulders, releasing the tension centered in his back. Then he smiled and said softly, "No. It was my fault. I shouldn't have used your home as a place to crash. I didn't mean to, but the bed seemed to pull me down." He looked at his watch again. "I was supposed to be in Austin an hour ago. That's why Mrs. Steinbeck called. They were checking to see if anything had happened to me."

"Oh." It was all Lacy could think of to say.

Sloan covered the space between them and took one of her hands, curling it into his own. "I'm sorry we were interrupted."

She didn't pretend to be coy. "So am I."

He remained still. "Lacy," he began slowly. "There's something I have to tell you. Only there isn't time now. What I have to say can't be rushed."

Lacy's heart did twin flip-flops. She remained silent.

"I have to go back to the hospital after work to see Jim. But I'd like to come by here afterward. Is that OK?" Allowing even that minute amount of truth its freedom lifted a little of the burden he had been carry-

ing. Everything would soon be out in the open where
he could deal with it.

Lacy searched his handsome features, her eyes running over his tousled blond hair and bronzed skin,
sensing the seriousness of his request. She agreed immediately.

"I may be late," he warned.

"I'll wait," she promised.

Sloan squeezed her hand and the loving smile he
sent her made Lacy's insides glow.

She followed as he moved into the hall. "You
haven't eaten anything yet. Could you stay a little while
longer? I'll make something quick. A sandwich won't
take long." She understood his need to leave, but she
didn't want him to go.

Sloan halted by the front door. "No," he decided.
"I'd better get out of here now. If I don't, it may be
another hour before I leave, and then Mrs. Steinbeck
will have to call again."

Lacy gave a tremulous smile, and Sloan bent down to
kiss the tip of her nose. Then he closed the door softly
behind him.

Lacy existed in a partial dream world for the following
couple of hours. All it had taken was one visit from
Sloan, and her life was back on an even course. At least
it was as even as it could be, considering the heights to
which her emotions were capable of taking her. Last
night she had been afraid, of exactly what she didn't
know. All she had was a name. But today, this morning, everything had changed. Possibly it was because
situations always seemed their worst at night. Possibly
it was because Sloan had come back to be with her and

if it hadn't been for the repeated interruption of the telephone they would have made love again.

Lacy was resting on the sofa where Sloan had earlier been sitting, Sampson curled beside her, the copy of the book he had given her in her lap. She ran her fingers over the hard cover and opened it to the beginning chapter. The first sentence she read concerned the unadulterated pleasure the author felt at getting into bed beside his wife—the warmth, the loving. And she sighed. What was Sloan wanting to talk with her about tonight? He had already told her that he thought he was falling in love with her, and she knew that she loved him. What was the next logical step? Was she being too old-fashioned in today's age to hope that he was going to propose?

Lacy's lips curved into a secret, happy smile. Yes, that had to be it. And what would she answer? Of course she would say yes! How long would he want to wait? Would a month be too long? She wanted Ariel to be back home and a part of the wedding plans. Possibly they could be married in this very house.

Her mind filled with plans. She would talk with one of her old professors, try to find a position similar to the one she had had in Boston. She didn't think it would be too hard. She was good at what she did. Finding another home in research wouldn't take long.

For some time Lacy sat staring at nothing, her imagination taking both herself and Sloan down the pathway of life, envisioning their eventual children, what their home life would be like. She even decided that she would take up hang gliding if she had to in order to share a part of what he liked to do.

The strident ringing of the telephone cut into her

happiness and brought her back to the everyday world. Previously, other than Ariel's early evening calls, the phone had barely rung. Now, today, it seemed to have come into a life of its own and she was beginning to hate it. Already there had been two wrong numbers, the caller having disconnected as soon as Lacy answered. She wondered if someone was playing a prank.

This time, when she made her way into the kitchen and lifted the receiver her answer was short, abrupt.

Again a silence greeted her. Then a muffled feminine voice grated into her ear,

"I'm only telling you this for your own good. Sloan Adams is going to marry Caroline Stanton. Leave him alone." Following an-other pregnant pause, there was a distinct disconnecting click.

Lacy stood there, unable to move. Nothing was real. She hadn't really heard what she had. This was just an extension of a dream—only it was rapidly becoming a nightmare. Had she heard the woman correctly? Lacy looked at the handset as if it contained an answer. But all along the words were echoing repeatedly in her mind. Sloan was going to marry Caroline. It was for her own good. Leave him alone. Sloan was engaged.

Starting to shake all over she replaced the receiver on its mount. No, she wouldn't believe it. It was just someone's idea of a sick joke. He couldn't be engaged. Not after the way he had been with her, not after the way they had made love. He wouldn't—he couldn't. He would have told her!

Or would he? Lacy didn't have a wide variety of experience with men. But she had heard some of her friends discussing the unfaithfulness of their ex-boyfriends and ex-husbands. About how they had found a likely prospect and strayed. Was that what she had been for Sloan? Was that all she had been?

She leaned against the kitchen counter as her trembling increased. Was that what he was wanting to talk with her about tonight?

But he had said he loved her!

No, someone was trying to make trouble. She wouldn't believe anything derogatory of Sloan, just on someone else's say-so. Especially when it was someone who was too cowardly to state her name, content to spread her poison anonymously. It was a lie. It had to be a lie. She would wait to hear what Sloan said himself.

Sloan arrived at the hospital that night to find that Jim was in much better shape than he had expected. He retained some paralysis on his left side, but it was minimal. The prognosis was that it would be relieved with time and a little physical therapy.

Sloan assured his partner that he and Max had been able to handle everything at the hospital and clinic, and would continue to do so until his return, that he was not to worry. Everything was under control. He left when Jim slipped into a healing nap.

Caroline moved quietly out of the room with him. Sloan looked at her tired expression and spoke softly.

"You should get some rest."

Caroline gave a small smile. "I will."

He felt at a loss for more words. He had never felt so ill at ease with Caroline before. Was it because what he knew he needed to tell her and what he could tell her were two different things? "Do you want me to drop you at your house? I'll wait if you want to stay longer."

Caroline shook her head. "No, I'm going to stay

here again tonight. The nurse said I could use the bed next to Dad's. She said she wouldn't tell." She paused, tenderness warming her expression. "Sloan, I don't know if I've ever told you this before, but you have to be one of the nicest people in the world."

Sloan felt like the worm he was. He shrugged off her compliment. "I wouldn't exactly say that."

"No, let me finish. I've wanted to say this for a long time and never got around to it. There were always other things to get in the way, and I got embarrassed. Sloan, I love you. There! I've said it!"

He wanted to run. He wanted to rush away and not hear. He didn't think he could stand hearing this, and then have to try to find a way not to hurt her too badly in the future.

She placed a hand on his arm, almost as if unconsciously she had read his desire for flight. "I've loved you since I was nine and you were eleven. When I was a teenager I had a crush on you to end all crushes, in case you didn't know. But now... what I feel for you is something so much more." Her blue eyes began to shimmer with tears. "I'm an only child. You are too. My mother died when I was eight, and you had all that trouble to live through with your father. Sloan, I don't feel like I'm an only child any longer. There was a time not long ago when I hoped—but things don't always turn out like you want them. Times change, people change." She drew a deep breath and wiped away an escaping tear. "Sloan, I guess what I'm trying to say— and not very well either—is that I don't think I could ever have a better brother than you. And if you'd tell me that you think of me in that way, too—as your real sister—you would make me the happiest person on this earth. I know Dad loves you like a son. Do you think we could make the family complete, a real one?"

Sloan was like an unmoving statue. He couldn't believe what he was hearing. What had happened? Was she saying that she loved him like a sister? He took a steadying step backward and Caroline's hand fell away. The shock she had given him was still making him mute.

Caroline looked at him in some concern. "Sloan?" she questioned anxiously.

He forced himself to answer. "I'd like nothing better, Caroline." His words were husky, and all the while he was saying them his mind was racing. She loved him like a sister! When had he gotten the story wrong? Was it all on his side that he thought they would eventually settle into marriage? He wanted to laugh. What a fool! *He* was the one with the wrong idea. And all this time he had been torturing himself about Lacy for no reason. He was a complete idiot!

Sloan wanted to shout his sudden happiness. But a hospital was not the place to attempt a jump over the moon. They might send him to the psycho ward and take measurements for one of those unfashionable little white coats. And with Caroline still standing there, traces of tears fresh in her eyes, he couldn't show just how ecstatic her words had made him. Nor could he show the gratitude he felt that the delicate woman he, too, now realized he loved in a brotherly way had removed the burden he had been carrying for what seemed to be forever. Somehow he held onto the vestiges of control until he could stumble from the hall, still dazed by what he had just learned.

This time he didn't hesitate to drive directly to

Lacy's home. He made the decision consciously. He had nothing to hold him back now. He would ask her to marry him. Yet was it too soon? He experienced a momentary qualm. What if she said no? His happiness faltered. Then he took his courage firmly in hand and set his jaw in an angle of determination. They had shared so much. If she wasn't ready to make a further commitment, he would wait. He would wait for as long as it took. Eventually, she would come to love him.

Because of his active sensitivity, Sloan could tell that something was wrong the instant Lacy opened the door. He subdued the desire to sweep her into his arms and instead pushed his hands deeply into the front pockets of his gray slacks.

Lacy backed away from the door, her gaze rising to give him one quick glance and then falling to the carpet. One look was enough. She ached to tell him of the call. She wanted to beg him to tell her that it was a lie. But she couldn't just blurt it out. What if he admitted that it was true?

She led the way into the living room in silence. Sloan had said nothing, and she couldn't seem to find the appropriate banal words. She motioned vaguely to the sofa and finally broke the quiet by saying, "Would you like to sit down?"

She was so stiff, so formal. Sloan gave his head a negative shake. He had the feeling he would rather face whatever was troubling her on his feet. She was so changed from the way she had been this morning. What could have caused it?

Lacy declined the position herself. She moved over to a side table and began to play with an empty vase that was sitting there.

Sloan kept his eyes riveted on her back. He had come with such high hopes. Now he was becoming afraid that they would not be realized. "Lacy?" he questioned.

She turned around slowly, her hazel eyes filled with hurt.

"What is it? What's wrong?" He suddenly wondered if something had happened to her sister, an accident of some sort.

"What makes you think something is wrong?" Lacy tried to put off the inevitable.

Sloan's heart sank. It wasn't her sister. It was something else. He started to move closer to her, but she backed away. He stopped, disquieted, a frown creasing his brow. "Something sure as hell is. Why did you back away from me just now?" The direct approach had always proved best in the past.

Her pulse speeded up. "Did I back away?"

He quickly erased the distance between them and took possession of one of her arms. "I want to know, Lacy."

She wouldn't meet his eyes. "Why don't you tell me what it is you wanted to say this morning and didn't have time for?" She was vibrantly aware of his nearness and had to fight to keep control of her emotions. But she had to give him his chance.

Sloan's teeth gritted. "I don't think it's all that important right now.

Lacy knew she was handling the situation poorly. But she couldn't change her approach. She had to know. "It is if it concerns Caroline."

Her quiet words sent a spear of ice through Sloan's chest. "Caroline?"

His grip loosened and she pulled away. She moved to

stand behind the sofa, almost as if she were using its bulk for protection. Lacy nodded. "Exactly what is Caroline to you, Sloan?"

"A friend," he answered quickly. Now he could say that without deceit.

Lacy's heart was pounding. She didn't want to continue, but she had to. "I had a telephone call that said differently."

Sloan let out a long breath. "Who?"

She gave an unstable laugh. "Aren't you even going to deny it?"

"I'm not going to waste my breath denying something when I'm not even sure what I'm accused of."

Lacy's fingers curled into her palms, her fingers cold in spite of the chaos in her veins. "She's much more than a friend to you, Sloan. Can you tell me that's not true?"

Now Sloan was becoming angry. He didn't like being grilled, not by anyone. And there was still that area of tenderness where he had lived with his own wrong assumptions over the past years. "No."

Lacy's head fell. It was true. Tears rushed into her eyes, but she blinked them away. She wasn't going to cry! Not in front of him. Instead she advised tightly, "I think you should leave."

Sloan's anger increased. "Why?"

"Because we don't have anything further to say to each other." She took a deep, steady breath. "I trusted you."

Sloan made as if to come around the sofa. He stopped when Lacy took another step away. Her look of pain assaulted him, but her continued withdrawal and her automatic presumption that he would leave willingly—like a lamb—made his tongue run away with his turbulent thoughts. "That's right. You trusted me," he repeated, "—enough to come to bed with me, to make love with me. And we would have made love again this morning if it hadn't been for the damn telephone!"

Lacy's face was flaming. "Don't!" She didn't need to be reminded.

"But you won't trust me now!" Maybe he was being unfair to her again. Technically he *had* betrayed her trust. The fact that his allegedly understood engagement was all a fabrication of his mind held no weight. But he hadn't set out to deceive her. It had just happened. And he had paid the price with his guilt. Wasn't that enough?

"Tell me you aren't engaged to Caroline!" Lacy was almost pleading. She wanted to believe him, trust him.

"I'm not."

"I don't believe you!"

"You'd rather believe whoever called?"

Stated in that manner Lacy knew she was crazy to side with the caller, but she was hurt. She had given herself freely to him. She loved him. And he had betrayed her.

She lifted her chin, her lips feeling frozen.

"I believe what you said earlier, when you admitted there was something more between you than mere friendship."

"You've got it wrong, Lacy," Sloan warned. "Almost as wrong as I did myself. But I know better now, and you would, too, if you'd just take the time to listen."

She didn't take even two seconds. As soon as the words left his mouth she challenged, "I want you to leave."

Sloan continued to look at her, anger and jealousy eating into his vital organs. "I could ask the same about you and that professor you worked with in Boston. What was he to you, Lacy?" The desire to inflict the same kind of hurt she was stabbing into him drove Sloan on. "Were the two of you lovers? Did you live with him, or did you just shack up on occasion before he died?"

Lacy drew in a shocked breath. "I never—shacked up—with him!" she denied, her face paling.

He gave a nasty laugh. "Sure. I bet." His eyes were like cold hard stones. "I believe that like you believe me!"

Lacy opened her mouth to protest again and then shut it. The more either of them said the more mired they became.

Sloan's gaze went over her, taking in her slightly disheveled hair and her pinched features. A fire seemed to light in the blue depths, burst into flame, and then be extinguished.

When he spoke again, his voice was dull, tired, as if the weight of the entire world had been suddenly inflicted upon his shoulders. "I'm probably making more of a fool of myself than I ever have before, but Lacy"—he paused—"I love you. I love you like I've never loved a woman before in my life. You may not believe it, and I may not deserve that you do, but it's true. It can't be changed."

After making the statement, he waited for some kind

of response. When none came he moved slowly into the entryway and then disappeared from view, leaving Lacy to stare into the empty space where he had been, her emotions a jumble of confusion.

Chapter Eleven

The time remaining before Ariel's return was interminable for Lacy. Over and over again Sloan's words repeated themselves in her brain. He had said that he loved her. He had said that the fact couldn't be changed. He had even denied being engaged to Caroline. But he wouldn't deny a special closeness to her. What was she to do? What did she believe?

She passed the days as best she could. Now that Sampson was well, she was free to leave the house for longer periods of time, so she spent more time in the University's library. She even paid a call on some of her old colleagues in the Biochemistry Department. But always in the back of her consciousness was her problem with Sloan. *Had* he only been using her?

She loved him, but she had been hurt very deeply by him. Sometimes the hurt seemed to overshadow everything else. More than once she wished that if this was what real love was like she had never discovered it. It was much safer to devote herself to the laboratory. There, there were variables, but their circumstances were controlled. Surprises were few and far between. Progress was made at a much slower pace.

Falling in love with Sloan had been the most quixotic thing she had ever done in her life. It had happened so fast. She hadn't even wanted to. But it was undeniable. And now the future looked so uncertain. She wasn't sure of anything anymore, and she didn't operate on any assumption beyond the moment she was living.

Sloan in the meantime was making life miserable for everyone around him. Not that he consciously meant to be irritable, he just was. With the animals entrusted to his care he was his usual gentle, caring self. With their owners, he was brusque. The only people he didn't show his displeasure to were Jim and Caroline. They didn't need more problems heaped on their already filled plates.

The first person to feel his wrath was Mrs. Steinbeck. Sloan knew she had to be the caller. She knew Lacy's number, she disapproved of his relationship with her, and she was a self-appointed keeper of the public's virtue. When he confronted her, he saw both the flash of triumph and the fear in her eyes. Had she thought he wouldn't be able to trace her? Was she secretly glad that he had? Did she think he wouldn't retaliate? Within five minutes Mrs. Steinbeck's two years at the hospital were at an end. And Sloan didn't care what his partners thought.

He hadn't needed to worry about Max's reaction, though, because the other vet heartily approved. He even volunteered his wife, who had been the previous office manager before the birth of their twins, as a substitute until they could find another person for the position.

Still, Sloan was miserable. He was angry with Lacy;

he loved her, but he wanted to shake her. He wanted to shake her until she would agree to listen to him. He knew everything was his fault. He knew he had been playing fast and loose with her, if looked at from her point of view. But if she would just listen, maybe then she would understand. Only she wouldn't listen. And he wasn't going to lower himself again to beg her. He might not like himself very much at the moment, but he did have some pride. If she wanted to talk with him, she was going to have to make the first move. He had been chasing her from the very beginning. Now it was her turn.

These bracing determinations were all well and good at the time they were made, and they carried him through most of his days. But as the second weekend approached since he had last seen Lacy, the stalwart ideals were beginning to fray a bit around the edges. Especially at night.

Ariel and David arrived home on a hot August morning. Ignoring their wishes Lacy met them at the airport. There was no sense in their paying for a taxi, not when she was so close and looking for something to occupy her time. She brought Sampson with her, and the greeting he gave his owners was something to behold. If Ariel had any worries left about his fitness, she was soon left in no doubt about his recovery. His small little body curled almost into itself as he jumped and yipped, and his tail nearly wagged itself loose.

Lacy's sister scooped the poodle up into her arms and after enjoying a host of dog kisses, laughingly handed him to her husband, who was the recipient of more.

Ariel then turned to Lacy. She hugged her sister to her. "I see what you said is true. It's hard to believe anything happened."

Lacy stepped back from the fragrance of expensive French perfume that Ariel was wearing. "He's made a fast recovery," she agreed, and next allowed herself to be momentarily enveloped by David's one free arm.

If a dog could beam, Sampson did. His bright little face looked overjoyed.

"He looks like he's been spoiled rotten," David teased.

Lacy raised her chin and returned in kind, "Not any-more than he's used to. When you're royalty, you ex-pect to be treated as royalty."

David laughed and glanced pointedly at his wife. His dark eyes that matched his thick black hair were twin-kling with mischief. "Sometimes I think his majesty, here, gets more in the line of service than I do!"

Ariel was suitably affronted. "That's not true! If any-one's been spoiled around here it's you. And I hope you don't expect me to continue the treatment." In an aside to Lacy she confided, "David's a pampered mess. All he's had to do for the last three weeks was pick up the phone, and his every wish has been granted."

David couldn't let the opportunity pass. "And all you've been doing is shopping! Lacy, can you believe this? We had to buy two more suitcases to bring all the junk home."

"Junk!"

"Whatever. All I hope is that it doesn't continue. We'll be in the poorhouse if it does."

"A woman has a first trip to Europe only once," Ariel answered with mock primness.

"Thank God," David teased.

His wife pretended to glare at him and then dissolved into a giggle. Lacy observed the banter between her sister and brother-in-law and knew that the trip had been good for them.

Ariel took Lacy's arm in hers as they began the walk to collect their luggage. "And how have things been with you, love? I know we talked frequently, but that was mostly about Sampson. Were you very bored?"

Lacy almost gave a short laugh, but she controlled herself. Bored? Was falling in love boring?

"No," she answered truthfully.

She felt Ariel's eyes examine her. "You don't look like you did when we left.'

Lacy gave a small smile. "I haven't changed."

"Something is different."

Lacy shrugged and changed the subject. "Tell me about Paris. I want to know all that you did, all that you saw."

Her ploy worked. Ariel had enough information to last until they got home, and she still had not left the French capital. She had London, Vienna, and Stockholm to go. But these David requested her to share later. What he wanted to do for the next few hours was sleep and suggested that she do the same, to help their bodies become reaccustomed to Austin time.

They excused themselves shortly, and once again Lacy was left on her own. She spent the time sitting curled on the sofa, at first glancing at and then reading the paperback romance Ariel had brought with her on the plane and had left sitting on the end table beside her purse. It was a British version of one of the more popular American series. The title caught Lacy's eye.

My Love Betrayed could have fitted her situation perfectly, and the story line, concerning an up-and-coming young defense lawyer who, years before, had discovered that she was being used by the unscrupulous district attorney with whom she had thought herself in love, and later met again, made Lacy read on. She wanted to see how the fictional heroine handled the situation, if she made a good job of directing her life.

When she was finished Lacy couldn't believe how caught up in the story she had become. There were some uncomfortable moments, especially in the love scenes, but she couldn't honestly say that she had not enjoyed it. The only thing that seemed unreal was the ending. Nothing could work out quite so easily. Nothing in real life, that was. After a serious misunderstanding, sometimes there was enough suspicion remaining to prevent a happy ending. In some instances people just did not get back together.

Lacy sighed and put the book aside, more depressed now than she had been when she started it. Maybe you had to be basically happy to enjoy reading a romance. Getting involved in other people's troubles when you were in a similar situation yourself was not exactly relaxing, or reassuring. Especially when the hero and heroine arrived at a conclusion so very different from what you feared would be your own.

Two days passed, days in which Ariel barely stopped talking long enough to breathe. Lacy was given a verbal tour of everything her sister saw, ate, and appreciated.

Finally, though, she at last exhausted her store of information and once again began to look at Lacy with concern. "Are you sure you're feeling all right?" Ariel asked, her brown eyes serious.

"Of course."

"You're not eating very much."

"I don't usually eat a lot."

Ariel frowned. "Your face is thinner. Have you lost weight?"

Lacy crossed her arms closer over her midsection, glad that they were sitting on the sofa. "I don't think so."

"Stand up. I want to see."

Lacy looked at her sister as if she had gone out of her mind. "Why? What difference does it make?"

"Because of the surprise I have for you. Now, come on. Stand up!"

Lacy did as she was directed and turned in a circle when Ariel whirled her finger in a tight spiraling motion. "Yes, I think it will still fit.'

"What?"

"The dress I bought for you in London. Remember? I told you about it the first time I called."

Lacy racked her memory. So much had happened.

"Come on. Into the bedroom."

She followed her sister into the master bedroom. Empty suitcases stood stacked in the corner and a number of bundles remained tightly wrapped.

"It will probably be a little wrinkled." Ariel withdrew one bundle from on top of a stack. "But we can fix that. She handed the package to Lacy, her brown eyes warm with love. "Here. Open it. I hope you like it."

Lacy sat on the edge of the bed. Another gift. Her fingers began to tremble as she remembered the last gift she had received. The book was still on her nightstand. She had read no more of it, but she kept it there as a test of her will. Her eyes became watery when she thought of Sloan—of her ache to see him again, to be held by him. Twice she had almost called him. What would it hurt to listen? But pride got in the way, pride and the fear that Caroline might be there with him. She knew she could never chance that. She would rather go on as she was now, with her suspicions, than learn that they were irrefutable fact.

"Lacy?" Ariel questioned when some time had gone by and she was still sitting there staring at the package.

She started. Her hazel eyes flew up to her sister's and then down to the parcel on her lap. Guiltily she tore through the paper. Inside was a dress like none she had ever owned. Made of a soft, flowing material in a warm shade of ivory, with touches of old-fashioned lace positioned at the neck, the bosom, and the ends of the sleeves, it was the kind of dress that came out of a fairy tale. She drew an appreciative breath.

Ariel smiled fondly. "I thought you'd like it."

"It's beautiful," Lacy whispered, her throat tightening. It could have been a wedding dress, it was so special.

Her sister came to sit beside her as she continued to stroke the delicate fabric. Ariel waited for a moment, then decided to plunge right in. "Lacy. Look at me."

Lacy bit her bottom lip. Ariel knew something was wrong and was determined to find out what it was. Lacy could tell by the sound of her voice. Yet she couldn't raise her head. She knew her emotions were too raw. If she was forced to talk about Sloan everything would come to the surface, and the carefully controlled facade she had been wearing for the world would collapse. Her eyes were awash with tears.

"Lacy. Please—" Ariel pleaded. "I'd like to help. I don't know what's wrong, unless—honey, is it that professor? Do you still miss him?"

A droplet escaped Lacy's eye and ran down over her cheek.

Ariel saw it. "Oh, baby. I'm sorry. I didn't realize—" She put her arm around her sister's shoulders and was silent a moment. Then she took a deep breath and said, "I have to admit I didn't think you really cared that much for him. I thought he was too old for you. That you were just infatuated with his intelligence, with his position. But I guess I was wrong." She paused to collect herself. Lacy's pain seemed so intense. "You really loved him, didn't you?"

Lacy heard what Ariel was saying. The words themselves meant little to her, but the sentiment did. Her sister was willing to share her hurt in order to help her. Lacy wanted to confide so terribly. Maybe it would help. She hadn't had anyone to talk to in so long.

She rubbed at the escaped tear, which had been followed by several more, and sniffed.

"I do love someone, Ariel. But it isn't Richard." She felt her sister's shock.

"Then who—?"

"I—it's someone you know."

Another shock. "Who?" This time the demand was more of an order.

"Sloan Adams."

"Sloan Adams?"

Ariel seemed flabbergasted.

"I love him," Lacy repeated.

Her sister began to recover some of her aplomb.

"Wait," she directed. "I don't understand. When did you meet him?"

"Don't you remember? When Sampson hurt his leg, Sloan was the vet I brought him to." While Ariel absorbed this information, Lacy went on. "But that wasn't actually the first time we met. We flew in from Boston together." She turned to meet her sister's wide gaze.

"You did?"

"He had been at some kind of convention."

"Why didn't you tell me? Was it a secret?"

"That I had flown in with him? No. I didn't really know who he was then. I knew he was a vet and that he came to Austin, but that was all."

Ariel was still another moment. "This is all rather sudden, isn't it?"

"Yes."

"Does—does he feel the same way about you?"

"He says he does."

Ariel sensed a problem. "So?"

"So-oh, Ariel!" Lacy cried. "It's all so confused. I've made a horrible mess of everything!"

Ariel hugged her sister's thin shoulders and looked on her with compassion. She remembered her own turbulent times with David.

"Well, I'm sure that with both of you admitting that you care for each other, there isn't much that can't be put right."

Lacy wished she could borrow some of her sister's optimism. Her chin lowered and she absently began to finger the dress's material once again. "There is if there's another woman on the scene."

Ariel's half-smile disappeared. "But I thought you just said that he loves you."

"I think he loves her, too. And I can't share, Ariel. Not at all. I didn't know I was so possessive until now. But I am."

Her sister was silent.

Lacy placed the package on the bed and stood up, needing to have some form of physical activity.

Ariel watched her agitated movements for several long moments before getting to her feet as well. She put a hand on her hip. "You know, Lacy, the members of our family have always done everything the hard way. We seem to have to get slapped down a few times before we learn, which means we don't always have an easy time of it with love. Remember how David and I almost broke up just hours before our wedding, not to mention the two times before that?" Lacy nodded. "And how Mom and Dad told us about their stormy courtship?" Lacy nodded again. "So what makes you think you'll be any different? A long time ago I came to the conclusion that we have to go through the hard times in order to appreciate the good. David and I have a happy marriage now. We don't always agree, but we love each other. And Mom and Dad were happily married for twenty-one years. So much so that everyone said they were almost relieved when they died together, because one would have been lost without the other." She paused and sighed. "I guess what I'm trying to get through to you is this: If you love Sloan, go get him. Fight for him if you have to. Don't let pride or anything else stand in your way. It's not worth it. Living alone with a lot of 'I could haves' isn't a good way to exist. At least make the effort. You'll never forgive yourself if you don't."

Lacy's back remained to her sister as she thought

about what she said. Then as she turned around, a light
began to glow in her eyes.

"Yes—yes, you're right." She thought to herself for
a moment, then said, "I'll do it!"

Ariel smiled her approval. "There's the old saying
about faint heart never winning a fair maiden. Well, it
applies the other way, too. Faint heart never wins an
available male."

Lacy reacted slowly. It was as if she was already con-
centrating on what she would say when she saw Sloan,
what she would do. Her smile came two beats behind
the time when it should have. "You're right again.'

"I know," Ariel agreed. "I usually am."

Lacy stiffened her shoulders in preparation for battle.
"I'd better go get ready."

"Would you like to wear this? It's a little fancy, but
it might help bring things down in your favor."

She followed her sister's motion to the dress. "No, I
have other plans for that if things work out the way I
want."

Ariel gave a small frown and then began to smile.
Neither sister voiced what was in her mind.

Finding Sloan proved to be more difficult than Lacy
had thought it would be. When she entered the veterinary hospital near Ariel's home, she was surprised at
the new friendly face that greeted her from the reception desk.

"Yes? May I help you?"

Did the woman find her behavior strange when she
came in without an animal and immediately began to
look toward the examination rooms as if expecting to
see someone?

"Ah—is Dr. Adams in, please?"

"Dr. Adams?" the woman repeated. She was much younger than the receptionist Lacy had met before. In her early thirties. Lacy wondered if she was a temporary.

"Yes."

"He's not here. I'm sorry. Could someone else help you?"

"Where is he?"

Some of the woman's friendliness disappeared. She looked Lacy over suspiciously.

"At our clinic in Austin," she finally divulged. "Look, if you have a problem, Dr. Dalton is here. Let me call him." She began to rise from her seat.

Lacy hurried to stop her. "No! It's all right. I'll go there." Then, at the startled expression on the receptionist's face, she tried to soften her adamancy with a smile. "I only want to see Dr. Adams."

The woman nodded, but Lacy could see her puzzlement.

"Thank you." She again tried for more normalcy.

"You're welcome," came the automatic reply. But Lacy knew she hadn't succeeded.

The drive into Austin almost caused Lacy to lose her nerve. She still wasn't sure what she was going to say. She wasn't even sure if she should be doing this. But Ariel's clear way of looking at the situation made it seem imperative that she at least try.

She slowed the car outside the clinic, taking in the well-remembered white exterior walls and the door that was the only physical obstacle between herself and Sloan.

Then she accelerated. She couldn't do it! If he had been at the hospital, she would have been able to rush into a credible explanation without a second thought. But here, now, after having had all this time to think, it was almost as if she were experiencing stage fright. Her stomach was tied in knots, her palms were sweaty. Her entire body felt at least five degrees cooler. She was afraid!

Lacy drove around the block three times, trying to regain some of her earlier confidence. What would it hurt? she asked herself. What was the worst he could say? Good-bye, get lost? She had as well as said those words to him.

If she had never stopped to think about it until now Lacy knew she had at last well and truly reached full maturity. No longer was she so much of an innocent in the ways of the world. She had loved a man, been loved by him, rejected him, and was now prepared to receive his rejection. Her resolve strengthened, and on the next swing around the corner, she directed the Buick toward the clinic parking area. If he didn't want to see her, she could take it. She would live. Not happily maybe, like the heroine in the book, but she would survive. And she would stay in Austin. It was the city of her birth, her sister and brother-in-law lived here, and there was an excellent university where she could find a job in research.

Her nervousness was well hidden when she entered the clinic. The last time she had done this, it had been to discover total confusion. This time, everything was quiet. The young woman behind the reception desk was reading a magazine and looked up only when Lacy pointedly cleared her throat.

"Is Dr. Adams in?" she asked, wanting to get the necessary over and done with.

"Yes, he is. Would you like to see him?"

Lacy drew a bracing breath. "Yes, please."

The receptionist nodded acceptance and pushed away from her desk.

The wait seemed endless to Lacy. Some of the coolness she had experienced earlier came back to attack her, and her stomach tried to rumble a protest. The symptoms were subdued only by force of will. She was not going to become a nervous wreck. She was not!

Footsteps came down the hall from Lacy's right. They sounded heavy on the linoleum flooring. They were a man's. She swung toward the doorway and was in time to see Sloan's emergence.

A dark scowl was on Sloan's face as he entered the waiting room. The clinic had been as quiet as a tomb all morning, no one seeming to have a need to bring in his pet. Then, as soon as he had decided to recheck the continued progress of a cat that had been found a week ago with all the signs of having gotten into some kind of chemical irritant—eyes swollen and runny, breathing sounding more like a wood-burning locomotive than anything alive—Jenny had come back to tell him that someone wanted to see him.

To say that he was not happy to be called away was a mild misstatement. But then, in fact, he didn't want to be here at all. He wanted to be out on some mountain, ready to soar into the sky, so that he could try to put from his mind all the troubling thoughts that had been bedeviling him. Yet what he really wanted was to be with Lacy.

Then, there she was, standing before him. He could

scarcely credit it. A multitude of emotions sped through him as he stopped short in his tracks.

She gave a tight smile. "Hello, Sloan."

Sloan hurriedly composed himself as best he could. "Lacy."

A tremulous smile tried to find purchase on her lips. "I was wondering if we might talk."

Was he dreaming? She wanted to talk? Scattered thoughts raced about his brain. "Here?"

Lacy looked around. "If you like."

Sloan steadied himself. They couldn't talk here. There wasn't enough privacy.

He took a deep breath, and Lacy's eyes narrowed. He seemed a bit taken aback. When she had first seen him, the frown he had been wearing had almost made her want to turn and run. He wouldn't want to listen. But she had stuck it out, and now began to wonder at his shaken reaction to her appearance.

"No, not here." He discarded his lab coat and gave it to the young receptionist. "Jenny, let's take an early break for lunch and try to be back for about one thirty. OK?"

Jenny's dark eyes almost worshiped his every word as she agreed. Lacy saw the look and felt her heart fall. Was this another woman she would have to fight against?

Once they were outside, Sloan hesitated. Then he started in the direction of his Jeep, which was partially hidden from view around a corner of the clinic. It was parked under a tree, with the windows rolled down so that the intense heat of day would not make it uninhabitable. Sloan saw Lacy into her seat and then came around to his.

"Where would you like to go?" he asked, keeping his eyes straight ahead.

Lacy said the first thing that came to mind. "Your place."

She felt Sloan's surprise. It was a moment before his hand came out to insert the key in the ignition. He never said a word in reply.

Traveling the same highway as she had so short a time before made Lacy wonder if she had suggested the right thing. In one way it was silly to leave the city. Ariel's car was back at the clinic; Sloan would have to return there in a couple of hours. But since he had given her the choice, his apartment was the only place she knew where they could talk and not be interrupted.

When they entered Sloan's apartment, Lacy carried through with her desire not to be interrupted. She walked to the telephone, removed the receiver from its rest, and dialed one number to engage it. She then moved to his sofa and sat down. Inside she was a trembling mass of insecurity, but she knew it was important that outwardly she look calm. She loved him and she was going to do her best to straighten out this horrible predicament. Several starting sentences flitted through her brain: Sloan, I've never done this before, but... Sloan, we need to discuss something... Sloan, I've been thinking, and... But none of them were right. Instead she chose to come directly to the point.

"You once told me you loved me. Did you mean it?"

Sloan took a seat in the chair beside her. "Why do you want to know?"

"Because it's important." Her eyes flashed upward and caught his. No emotion showed in either face.

"Why is it important?"

"Just answer my question."

"After you answer mine."

Lacy moved uncomfortably. He was after his pound of flesh. "Because it means a lot to me."

"Why?"

He was impossible. "It just does!"

Sloan leaned back in his seat. "I meant it."

Lacy swallowed. She had almost missed his admission in expectation of having to retaliate. "As much as you do Caroline?" She plunged right in. She had to know his answer. Everything hinged upon it.

Sloan's blue eyes moved over her face and hair and on down to the pale blue dress she was wearing. He loved every inch of her, every molecule. Excitement was beginning to surface deep within him. "I love you more."

Lacy expelled a long breath. She had gotten what she came for. "Then why—?"

Sloan sat forward, cutting off her question. He reached out for her hands and drew her toward him. Lacy moved until she was on the edge of the seat, their interlaced fingers spanning the short distance between them.

"Lacy, Caroline and I aren't engaged. We never were," he explained earnestly, then gave a deprecating smile. "A lot of people, including myself, thought that we were. But it turns out the lady thought differently."

"*She* thought differently?"

Sloan nodded. "It's a pretty long story," he warned, but at her encouraging look he continued. "Caroline and I grew up together. Her father is one of my partners, and he's always been like a father to me. He took me on, mostly out of pity, I believe, when my real father left. He gave me a job at his office, at the clinic. He helped pay my way through A&M and took me back under his wing again when I graduated. Caroline and I—well, I decided that we'd probably marry one day and took it for granted that she did too. And, I have to be honest, I was still under that impression when I met you. It was just recently that I learned the truth." He looked deeply into her eyes. "It came as quite a relief. I didn't want to hurt her, but I would have if it had come to a choice between you. I want you, Lacy. No one else. Even if Caroline and I had really been engaged, I would have had to tell her. Marriage isn't something you go into loving someone else."

"No, it isn't," Lacy agreed, her heart starting to pound. It was all coming right! She had said the right thing. Done the right thing.

Sloan looked at their mingled fingers and rubbed his thumb along hers. Then he slowly raised his gaze, and the magnetic drawing they had both experienced from their first encounter began to cause the air to sizzle between them. Sloan's fingers convulsively tightened, and a sensuous smile came to play around his lips.

Lacy's breath shortened and her entire body began to tingle. Sloan had never looked so handsome or so dear. She knew they were on the verge of something wonderful.

His voice was like thick, warm honey when he said softly, "I love you, Lacy. I want to marry you."

She wondered if mere words could cause such ecstasy. Her hazel eyes began to shine. "Oh, yes, Sloan. Yes!"

A current of happiness shot through Sloan's being. Everything had looked so bleak just a short hour before. How could so few minutes change an entire life?

He didn't waste time with more conversation. He stood up and pulled Lacy with him. He needed to feel the reality of her against him. Lacy went willingly, loving the hard masculine strength he possessed, loving the faint tinge of spicy aftershave and the stronger scent that was his. She never wanted to part from him again. She had missed him so!

Like two lovers who had been separated by miles instead of minds, they came together, straining to avoid even the most minute chance that they would be torn apart again.

Lacy could hardly believe that this was happening. Yet as his hands began to stroke the curve of her waist, and her own fingers curled into the denim shirt that covered the muscles of his back, a searing fire more intense than any she had ever expeienced before made her wholly aware that they were truly in each other's arms. Their mouths hungrily sought and found each other. Then, as naturally as nature's design decreed, Sloan lifted her into his arms and took her to his bedroom.

What followed was more intensive instruction for Lacy. When they had come together before, she thought she had reached the ultimate in physical appreciation. Now she found that she had not. Sloan's lovemaking was slow and steady, as he kept a forcible restraint on himself in order to allow her to attain the same explosive level of desire that he himself would reach.

The warmth of his skin against hers—his clothing having been discarded carelessly on the carpet beside her own—the drugging intensity of his kisses, the touch of his sensitive fingers over every portion of her body—Lacy had known nothing like it! Her body quivered, her soul cried out, as the quest for full enjoyment came nearer to its goal.

Then, finally, the wonderful agony burst, and when she called out her primal need, her voice came from the fog-enshrouded world of pure sensation. She had scaled the inexpressible heights of pleasure. She had attained her goal.

In that moment, shuddering his delight, Sloan released his hold on himself and joined her, losing himself to the assuagement of both body and spirit.

Their joy, their rapture, knew no limits.

Sloan rested against her for a moment, coming down reluctantly from the beauty of the ultimate expression of the love they shared. A sheen of perspiration was spread lightly on his skin, and his breathing was rapid and erratic. The feel of her body lying beneath him, still a part of him, was profound. He dropped a soft kiss on the inside of her neck, tasting the fine drops of her perspiration that had collected there. Then he rolled onto his side, hugging her to him, not wanting even now for the smallest measure of space to separate them.

Lacy lay spent against him. Never had she known such wonder. Her happiness knew no bounds. Her cheek was pressed against the curve of his neck, her head resting on his shoulder, their bodies intertwined. She could hear the strong beats of his heart and feel the sensitive warmth of his skin. And in that moment she vowed that she would never love another. Her life was to be forever blended with Sloan's. What he did, where he went, she would follow.

A warm kiss was delivered to her naked shoulder and she raised her vision to meet the love evident in his gaze.

"You know," he teased huskily, "we're going to get good at this if we keep trying."

Lacy's hazel eyes widened, and then as she understood his meaning, they crinkled with humor.

"Then, by all means, we should keep trying," she agreed.

Obviously Sloan approved of her willingness, because he bent his head and took her lips in a kiss of such sweet intensity that Lacy was once again lost to everything in the world but him.

When he lifted away, his expression was one of complete happiness. He looked down into her beloved face, and the love inside him expanded and grew until he didn't think there would be more room. How was it possible that he had stayed away from her this long? He was an idiot, a total idiot! He had thought himself one before; now it was unarguable. Only a fool would allow stupid pride to get in the way of happiness. He could only hope that he would have broken down eventually. His eyes traveled from her mouth to the beautiful swell of her breasts, and he felt something inside him quicken and twist. If there was one thing he had learned from all of this, it was that he was never again going to let anything come between them. Never.

Lacy was aware of his heated gaze going over her and hugged to herself the fact of her undoubted ability to stir him. She ran her fingers down along his arm from his shoulder to his elbow, appreciating the feel of him, tantalizing them both by her action.

Sloan took revenge by cupping a breast and gentling it.

Lacy drew a tremulous breath. "I do love you so very much, Sloan. I really do."

"And I love you, Lacy. I can't seem able to stop."

"Do you want to?" She met his look.

"I'd rather die."

Lacy smiled and put her fingers on either side of his head, pulling him to her, enfolding him as a mother would a child—cherishing him. "So would I," she promised softly.

Sloan lay quiet for several moments, then he asked, "Would you hate it if we can't take our honeymoon right away?"

Lacy released him and he lifted away until he could see her face. "No," she replied, watching him levelly.

Regret darkened his returning look. "It may be some time. With Jim out Max and I have our hands full. It could be several months."

"You mean we're going to have to wait that long to be married?"

A slow smile curved Sloan's lips and deepened the small network of expression lines beside his eyes. "Is that too long?"

"Yes."

Her quick answer had Sloan laughing. "That's what I like, an honest woman." Then his humor lessened and he tipped her chin upward. "It's too long for me, too. I'd like to get dressed right this minute and head into Austin to find a judge. But I think there's something that might slow us up, like a license test. Would tomorrow be too soon?"

Lacy began to smile. "Morning or evening?" she

challenged. There was no rush; she was confident of him, of their love. And she knew that the marriage ceremony was just that: a formality couples went through to legalize their love, with only a little piece of paper to show for its performance. Yet it was a function that she wanted to follow. She wanted to be a part of Sloan in every way possible.

"Evening. I know it's not very romantic for me to say that, but there's the clinic to think about. I can't leave Max to take care of both."

Lacy mentally bit her lip. She was marrying a doctor, and even if he was an animal doctor, there were sacrifices she was going to have to make. All aspects of the medical profession demanded them.

"Evening will be fine." She looked at him curiously. "Are you going to tell Caroline?"

Sloan touched her lips with his, as if he had gone much too long without doing so. "Sure. And she'll come. She's part of my family. We'll have to go by and see Jim, too. Will that be OK with you?"

"Of course. I'm looking forward to meeting him."

"And not Caroline?" Sloan seized upon her omission.

"Caroline most of all. I want to meet the woman who was silly enough not to keep you when she had the chance."

"She may consider that she had a lucky break," Sloan advised humorously.

"Then that's her problem," Lacy returned callously. "I think she's insane."

Sloan smiled, then a reflective light entered his eyes as he said,

"Lacy—"

She waited, listening for what it was that had suddenly come to trouble him.

But he changed his mind. As he looked down at her, at the way her nose tilted ever so slightly, at her delicately drawn lips, at the clearness of her eyes, he couldn't do it. His curiosity about her past—about the professor she had worked with—could wait. He was jealous no longer. He knew he had her love now. He was not going to ask for more. Maybe one day, when she felt like it, she would tell him. Until then, it wouldn't matter.

"What?" she questioned, wondering at his hesitation.

Quickly Sloan improvised. "As much as I want to, we can't stay here much longer. I have to go back to the clinic. I told Jenny one thirty, and it's almost that now."

Lacy glanced at her wrist watch. Like him, it was the only article she wore. "Yes—I see."

A whiff of perfume wafted more strongly with her movement, and Sloan gave a muffled groan.

"To hell with being back at one thirty. I'll get there when I get there. If there's an emergency, Jenny knows how to get in touch with Max."

She held a palm to his chest preventing his pulling her closer. "Are you sure?" she asked. She didn't want him to do something he might regret later.

Sloan gazed at her with melting heat. He wanted her. He couldn't seem to get enough of her. But rationality told him that his place was back at the clinic. And after fighting a monumental battle with his desires, he gave a short laugh and conceded. "No."

Lacy had been busy with her own struggle. If he had

continued with his action she would have given in. But when he did not, she found strength enough to win herself.

"We'd better get dressed then," she suggested.

Sloan nodded but made no move. Then as she sat forward, ready to swing her feet from the bed, he stopped her and drew her back.

"Yes," he whispered, changing his previous reply, before covering her lips and destroying any of what little resolve she had left.

It was closer to two thirty before Sloan and Lacy reappeared at the clinic. And that was to find that only one person had dropped in, and he was perfectly willing to wait while Sloan saw Lacy to her Buick.

"I don't want you to leave," Sloan said huskily as he bent to where she was seated behind the wheel of the car.

Lacy looked up at him with love-laden eyes, the little slashes of yellow that intrigued him very much in evidence.

"I'll be waiting for you," she whispered.

"If things don't pick up, I may shut down early."

"All right."

Words seemed so inadequate. Lacy brought his head nearer and directed her lips to his. For a long moment, speech was unnecessary. Then they broke apart.

"If I could get rid of Mr. Rodriguez, I'd shut down now," Sloan admitted thickly, half in jest, half in seriousness.

"No, you do what you have to," Lacy replied, although she was decidedly tempted. "If we're going to be married tomorrow evening I have a few things to do myself."

"Like find the right dress?" he guessed, smiling, mentally running over his own choice of clothing for such a special occasion. Even if theirs wasn't going to be a spectacular event, because they chose expediency over pomp, he wanted it to be perfect.

Lacy smiled softly. "No, I've already got something exactly right. Ariel brought it to me as a present from her trip."

"Then what?"

She liked his smile—no, she loved it! And his nose was perfect too. Had it been only a month since she had first seen him? It seemed much longer.

"Oh." She waved a hand. "All sorts of things. Hair, nails, things like that."

Sloan grinned. "Yeah, I think I know what you mean. There are a few people I want to tell, too."

Lacy laughed outright. "Will I ever be able to fool you?"

"I doubt it. I knew from the first moment we met that you were going to be pretty special in my life.

Lacy continued to look at him. "But you left! And you didn't even know my name!"

"That's true. Maybe I should amend that to say I knew you *could* be pretty special in my life."

"Is that why you hurried away so fast?" she wondered.

"It might be."

"And after saying such a perfectly horrible thing— that about it not having been nice to meet me."

A devilish light appeared in Sloan's eyes. "That really got to you, didn't it?"

"No," Lacy denied quickly, seeing his trap. Then she admitted, "Yes."

"Why?"

"Because of the way I was feeling. I was aware of everything about you."

"Love at first sight?" he suggested.

"No, I wouldn't call it that," she answered honestly, thinking how long it had been before she could come near to calling it that.

"Me, either," he agreed. "On my side it was more like lust at first sight."

Lacy met his teasing gaze, made a face, and pushed him away. "Go back to work, Dr. Adams. Your patient is waiting."

Sloan laughed, the crazy happiness that had taken hold of him making him feel as if he owned the entire world. "All right. But I'll be at your sister's as soon as I possibly can."

Lacy sparkled, a reflection of the beauty-filled universe. "All right, that's a date!"

Only to have Sloan contradict, "No, my love, that is a promise."

The sleek jet's aisles were crowded with passengers filing on board. Some were on vacation, others were traveling on business, and still others were going to see faraway loved ones. All were moving along to find their seats. Some were irritable, some were laughing, some were stony-faced with boredom. But none were quite as happy as the couple already occupying two seats on the forward left side of the airplane. Anyone could see that they were happy. One look at their faces could easily convince even the most devoted disbeliever. And yet they seemed to be arguing.

"That's not going to fit," the man could be heard to

say testily. "You'll have to put it in the compartment
above."

"I would, dear, if you hadn't crammed all of your
things inside," the woman answered with saccharin-
coated venom.

"Well, there are plenty of others if you'd just try and
find one."

"I'm waiting for all the people to pass," came the
retort.

The man made an irritable noise deep in his throat
and then started to chuckle, which caused the woman
to break into infectious laughter. An observer could be
forgiven his puzzlement.

Sloan's blue eyes watched his wife as she finally
managed to slide the satchel she insisted on carrying on
board under the seat ahead.

"There!" she cried proudly. "See, I told you it
would fit!" Lacy met her husband's gaze, and an un-
ashamed glow of love shone from her eyes.

As he had warned, their honeymoon trip had had to
be postponed for a time. But the length of time wasn't
nearly as bad as he had thought. They had been married for only a month and were already on their way to
New York, and from there on to England where they
wanted to see some of the Yorkshire countryside that a
certain English veterinarian had written of so warmly.

Sloan reached out to touch Lacy's cheek. No man
could have managed to fall into such luck as he, he
thought. To have found a woman like Lacy, all warm
and loving and giving, not to mention intelligent. For
their return in three weeks time she had already lined
up another position, at the University of Texas, doing
research on a project similar to the one she had previ-

ously studied. A professor there had gladly accepted her on his staff. Sloan was proud.

Also, he was relieved. Lacy had told him about Richard Evans, and the last vestiges of any jealousy that might have remained disappeared completely, never to see light of day again. Her divulgence seemed to complete their union.

Lacy turned her cheek and kissed her husband's hand, smiling as she looked across at him. Ariel had been thrilled at their marriage because of her knowledge of Lacy's affection. Then, later, after getting to know Sloan on a more personal level, she had confided to Lacy that she couldn't have picked better for her herself, which meant that Sloan would forever bear her stamp of approval.

Dreamily Lacy remembered her wedding. The ivory dress had been perfect. So had the brooch Ariel had given her to go with it, a present she had withheld at the time of gifting Lacy with the dress because, Ariel-like, she had wanted to extend her pleasure. As well, she had endowed Lacy with an exquisite French perfume. But Sloan had since told her that he much preferred her own, so Lacy hadn't brought the more expensive bottle with her on this trip. Their month of marriage had been perfect, a continuing celebration of their love. And she could think of no better news than they had received the previous week, which told them Jim was now ready to resume a part of his work and that the partners were going to admit another vet into their practice. Lacy had been happy for Jim because of his recovery and happy for the new partner, John McNeil; but, most of all, she had been thrilled for herself and Sloan, because now they would have a great deal more free time to spend with each other—and they could also make plans for their postponed honeymoon.

Sloan felt the accustomed rush of heightened desire sweep through him the instant Lacy kissed his hand, and he wished they were not on the plane. But then for the next three weeks they had nothing better to do than be with each other, an idea he was looking forward to with increasing excitement.

But for one moment he surrendered to a curious introspection and asked softly, "Lacy? Do you have any regrets?" He didn't think that she did, but suddenly it seemed important for him to know.

Lacy crossed her arm over his and reached up until her soft palm was against the curve of his cheek.

"None. Do you?"

"Only that I didn't meet you sooner."

An amused light sparkled in her eyes. "What? And miss all the fun we had?"

Sloan groaned and dropped his hand, causing hers to drop as well. "You call that fun?" he demanded incredulously. "I was in misery almost all of the time! I wanted you so badly and felt so darned guilty about Caroline!"

"And well you should," Lacy concurred with mock sternness. "She's such a nice person."

"I couldn't help it," Sloan shrugged.

"Was I that irresistible?" Lacy teased.

"I had to fight with myself every time I saw you to keep from jumping your bones."

"Sloan!"

"Well it's true."

Lacy pretended to be prim. "I think that's scandalous."

"And exactly how did you feel?"

"About what?"

"About me." He didn't let her get away with pretended ignorance.

"I wanted to jump your bones too," she admitted, and then giggled at his feigned attempt to attack her.

Sloan relaxed against his seat and threatened, "Just you wait till I get you alone!"

Lacy impishly challenged. "And what will you do?"

"I think you already know," Sloan answered meaningfully, enjoying the game by letting his gaze run hotly over her. He pretended to twirl an invisible mustache.

"Will I want to scream for help?" she asked curiously.

"Well," Sloan answered, a true hunger rising up to replace his banter. "You may want to scream, but I don't think it will be for help."

Lacy's hazel eyes twinkled in anticipation. "Is that a threat?" she persisted.

"No, my dear, *that* is a promise."

In spite of the crowded conditions around them Sloan leaned over and drew Lacy into his arms, his mouth covering hers in a kiss that held, as he had said, a wealth of promises, which would be collected over the space of their lifetime together.

HARLEQUIN *Love Affair*

Now on sale

DESERT FIRE   *Rebecca Flanders*

Trucker Camp Campbell rescued Dusty Macleod as she was fighting off three amorous teenagers in the middle of the Nevada desert. Homeless and penniless, Dusty possessed nothing but a fiery temper and a secret dream of a house with a willow tree. As they travelled the highway to Arizona, Dusty was able to conceal her worry and fear beneath complaints about the constant trucker music that blared from Camp's tape deck.

Yet when they reached Flagstaff, it was hard for Dusty to leave that music, and even harder for her to choose between her dreams and the safety of Camp's company. . .

PASSION'S PREY   *Ginger Chambers*

Dr. Sloan Adams provoked Lacy Stewart endlessly. Trapped beside the annoyingly handsome veterinarian on the flight from Boston to Austin, Texas, Lacy only wanted to be left alone. Sloan Adams was by turns infuriating and exasperating.

Lacy breathed a sigh of relief when the flight was over but, as luck would have it, their paths crossed again . . . and again.

It wasn't love. Love was that calm, comfortable feeling Lacy felt for Richard Evans. Sloan Adams didn't make her feel comfortable. In fact, he made her feel like running in the other direction. But then, Lacy kept asking herself, why wasn't she running?

RIVER RAPTURE   *Vella Munn*

When Michon volunteered to chaperon a group of teenagers on a trip down the John Day River, she knew her appearance worked against her. Employed by an exclusive department store in Oregon, Michon felt pressured to look model-perfect all the time. But the real Michon ached to be set free. In fact, Michon hoped this trip would reveal her true self, and in Chas Carson, the magnetic owner of Carson River Tours, she finally found someone she thought could help her.

Next month's titles

THE LAST KEY *Beverly Sommers*

After eight years, Toby had almost stopped expecting him. Hidden away in Key West, running a charter fishing boat, Toby had changed her hair, her clothes—even her walk. But when she saw Mac McQuade, she knew she had never been safe.

Toby. No birth certificate, no fingerprints on file, no identification at all. But Mac thought he knew who she was. She wouldn't slip through *his* fingers. Funny, she didn't look the type—her proud, determined spirit fascinated him. Yet lives were at stake and his duty was clear. He had to bring her in!

WINTER'S BOUNTY *Muriel Jensen*

The Christmas reunion in Astoria, Oregon, was a boisterous gathering of love in many forms, but Marijane Westridge was a stranger to all of them. Her mother's recent wedding, her older sister's tempestuous marriage, her younger sister's irresponsible affection for her child—all left Marijane bewildered.

At least until she looked at James Sullivan's love for his adopted son and beheld a kindred spirit. James radiated the kind of love that increased joys and lessened sorrows. Marijane had only to take his hand to share a lifetime of that wonderful emotion . . .

CHEROKEE SUMMER *Anne Henry*

Jordan Marshall's days, divided between her job and her graduate-school courses, had fallen into a dull routine and the archaeological dig near Seneca, Oklahoma, held the irresistible promise of ten weeks' excitement.

The reality of the excavation was a shock—blistering sun, back-breaking work, the most primitive facilities imaginable . . . and Professor Paul Nicolle.

Paul Nicolle, who had expected a male student, angrily implied that Jordan was a starry-eyed incompetent. Jordan refused to be intimated. She would do her share, she promised him. But silently she prayed she would survive the ordeal . . .

These two absorbing titles
will be published in May
by

HARLEQUIN
SuperRomance

THE AWAKENING TOUCH by Jessica Logan
Jan Jordan had spent all her life in the peaceful
isolation of her mountain home in Maine. Even in
her wildest dreams she could never have imagined a
man as compelling as Jason Farrell.

Jan had helped rescue the wealthy businessman's
son, but Jason felt more than gratitude. He wanted
her to leave her home and go with him. He wanted
her.

She knew his ex-wife's betrayal had left him bitter.
Love no longer had a place in Jason's life—only
passion. Yet still a powerful force drew Jan to him.
If only things could be different. If only . . .

LITTLE BY LITTLE by Georgia Bockoven
The former weather girl no longer brought disaster
to the job. She was an incisive reporter now—and
an exciting woman.

When NASA spokesman Mike Webster tried to get
close to Caroline Travers, she backed off. Her
ex-husband had shown her the selfishness of love;
she wouldn't risk humiliation again.

But Mike was one to give, not take. Forced to
abandon his dream of space flight, all he craved was
a home with Caroline. Mike was warm and sexy,
honest and altogether lovable, and Caroline was
sorely tempted to believe in him . . .

HARLEQUIN
Love Affair
Your Chance to Write Back!

We'll send you details of an exciting
free offer from Harlequin Love Affair,
if you can help us by answering these
few simple questions.

Just fill in this questionnaire, tear it out
and put it in an envelope and post
today to:

Harlequin Reader Survey,
FREEPOST,
P.O. Box 236,
Thornton Road,
Croydon, Surrey. CR9 9EL
You don't even need a stamp.

Please note:
READERS IN SOUTH AFRICA
write to
Harlequin S.A. Pty., Postbag X3010,
Randburg 2125, S. Africa.

P.T.O.

What is the title of the Harlequin Love Affair you have just read?

. . . .

How much did you enjoy it?

Very much ☐   Quite a lot ☐   Not very much ☐

Would you buy another Harlequin Love Affair book?

Yes ☐   Possibly ☐   No ☐

How did you discover Harlequin Love Affair books?

Advertising ☐   A friend ☐   Seeing them on sale ☐
Elsewhere (please state)

. . . .

How often do you read romantic fiction?

Frequently ☐   Occasionally ☐   Rarely ☐

Name (Mrs / Miss)   . . . .

Address   . . . .

. . . .

Postcode   . . . .

Age group: Under 24 ☐   25-34 ☐   35-44 ☐
45-55 ☐   Over 55 ☐

LA1